MW01088636

Point of Honor

The Exiled Fleet Book 4

Richard Fox

Copyright © 2019 Richard Fox

All rights reserved.

ISBN: 9781710042900

Chapter 1

Alarms blared around Commodore Gage as he stared hard into the holo tank. A Cathay fleet bore down on the *Orion* and the rest of the last free Albion ships. The ship's sensors read active target lock from the Cathay and their torpedo ports were open and ready to fire.

Price, his executive officer, looked at him through the holo. "We have requests from several of our captains to change our formation—at least get up to speed so we can maneuver if this does turn into a shooting match," she said.

"I don't believe the Cathay want a fight," Gage said.

"They've got a funny way of showing it," she said. "Cathay ships are normally designed to favor a torp load-out over cannons. They're approaching the outer edge of the engagement envelope, and if we don't—"

"Hold position," he said. "No hostile acts."

Glancing first at the bridge crew, she leaned forward into the holo. "Commodore, this isn't like Sicani. These are Kong ships of the line, not a bunch of pirates that are as likely to fire on each other as they are to shoot at us."

A hail appeared in the tank from the Reich battleship that had travelled through slip space with the Albion fleet. Gage raised a finger to tap a button and open a channel, but hesitated. He moved his hand to one side and expanded a news-feed window showing Albion—or what appeared to be Albion—ships firing on Cathay vessels.

"Gunnery," he called out to the bridge, "any more on this video? Can you confirm those are our ships?"

"Target analysis suggests those are the *Thames* and the *Sedgewick*," Lieutenant Clarke said. "Both ships from the 5th Fleet anchored at Sandov."

"That's not helping us," Gage said as he leaned against the control ring and glanced at the still unanswered hail from the Reich ship *Castle Itter*.

"Unter-Duke Klaven might help us," Price said, pointing at the hail. "I can take it if you—"

Gage shook his head.

The incoming Cathay ships spread out and changed course, bringing their port sides to cross the prow line of the *Orion* in a few minutes, leaving the ship open to a devastating barrage if Gage and his fleet didn't react quickly.

"Captain Jensen's in command of the *Thames*," Gage said.

"Sir...the Kongs?" Price asked nervously.

In the holo, the Reich battleship lumbered forward and crossed over the top of the Albion formation, situating itself between the Cathay line of fire and the *Orion*.

The hail from Klaven closed.

"Get me the *Arjan Singh*," Gage said. The Indus cruiser had held back since the combined fleet had arrived in the Lantau system, well away from the threat the Cathay posed.

"Captain Birbal is on another line," Price said, "according to this very polite message from the Indus ship."

"As expected," Gage said. "He's on the horn with the Cathay commander…Governor General Han, was it?" He opened up an intelligence directory and read what little had been collected on the man before the Daegon invaded.

The alarms ceased as the Cathay ships stopped targeting the *Orion*. The system defenders slowed their velocity and began turning back to Lantau.

A hail from the *Castle Itter* reappeared, this time with two joint callers.

"Don't stand down just yet," Gage told Price and opened the line.

Klaven, Birbal, and Han appeared in the holo, the head and shoulders of each man in its own window.

"Birbal and I have talked some sense into the locals," Klaven said, crossing his arms over his chest.

"You made it quite clear that I'd have to

shoot my way through your ship to get at the Albion," Han said. "The Cathay Empire has no hostile intent toward the Reich."

"Smart move, I assure you," Klaven said.

"The Reichsman and I have vouched for you and your fleet, Regent Gage," Captain Birbal said.

"Regent?" Han sneered. "There's no Gage in the Albion royal line. You've fallen for a pretender."

"Now that we've decided that we're not going to shoot our way to an understanding," Gage said, "can we discuss a number of other issues? I am the regent. Albion doesn't need to clear that with the Cathay."

"Albion fights alongside the Daegon!" Han shouted. "I was there when your ships opened fire on us at Taisan. Did your kingdom invite the invaders to your doorstep or did you cower like a scolded dog the second they opened fire?"

Gage's face hardened and one side of his mouth quivered.

"Gentlemen!" Klaven raised his hands. "Believe it or not, we're all on the same side here—as confusing as things may be. Let's save that ire for the green or blue bastards, yes?"

"Gage's actions and history are well-known to us," Birbal said. "They've shed blood fighting the Daegon beside my people. Do not insinuate otherwise, Han."

"Put yourself in my position," Han said. "This system's security is my responsibility. A hostile force arrives and—"

"Who's hostile?" Klaven asked. "*I'm* not hostile. Gage isn't hostile. Our Indus friend here certainly isn't hostile. Why don't we take a moment and figure all of this out with the Albion—apparently Albion—ships you have on video."

"Klaven, you're vouching for the Albion's behavior?" Han asked. "Your own personal guarantee?"

"You want me on record to blame if you open fire on the *Castle Itter* at the same time you attack the Albion? Clever, Han. You don't want to keep the Reich from a legitimate *casus belli* against the Cathay. A legitimate request. And fine, I take full responsibility for Gage's conduct in system."

"As do I," Birbal said.

"Agreed." Han's eyes narrowed. "You three are the senior-most representatives of your star nations in this system. Come to the Autumn Palace at sunrise. One shuttle each. Minimal security. This is a League meeting."

Han's window closed and his fleet turned back to the planet in the holo.

"We've received anchor coordinates," Price said. "Decent standoff from Lantau."

"They're keeping us at arm's length," Gage said. "This is progress, at least."

"There," Klaven said, running fingers through his hair, "that wasn't so bad now, was it?"

"The Cathay invited us to the palace." Birbal stroked his long, dark beard. "This is out of the ordinary for them, yes? The palaces are sacred to their emperor."

"There are two Golden Fleet ships in orbit…" Gage said.

"We live in interesting times," Klaven said. "Isn't that what the Cathay like to say? One of their curses, yes? I'm bringing my Genevan. You doing the same?"

"Better safe than sorry," the Commodore said. "Though I've been to worse places with just Thorvald at my side."

"These aren't your run-of-the-mill pirates." Klaven ran his palms down his uniform. "Dress to impress."

Birbal nodded and both commanders vanished from the holo tank.

"I can't believe those are our ships, sire," Price said. "Maybe the Daegon have their own crews in the ships. Worst case."

"It could be worse, XO. Much worse," Gage said. "Getting the League behind a liberation offensive just got harder...but I'll get answers from the Kongs. Even if the truth isn't what we want to hear. Thorvald?"

Gage turned to the Genevan guard standing against the bulkhead. Thorvald leaned forward slightly at the waist, the light behind the T on his visor growing brighter.

"I...I will coordinate with local security," Thorvald said. "Just yourself, sire?"

"Prince Aidan stays aboard the *Orion*," Gage

said. "We're not going to risk another Madras."

"Understood," Thorvald said.

"Price," Gage said, "ready the court martial proceedings for Arlyss. I want that matter dealt with as soon as I return from Lantau."

Price nodded and Gage left the bridge.

Chapter 2

Pain.

Seaver's entire world was pain. White-hot nerves up and down his body. His spine aflame. Eyes burning with white light. He wanted to scream, but his jaw was clamped shut and his chest wouldn't move, his lungs full of air but unable to breathe on their own.

Through the agony, he felt a presence, a shadow of light behind the never-ending flood of white assaulting his optic nerves.

Mom?

The pain vanished, as if his torturer had flipped a switch on his suffering, and his body went slack. His eyelids twitched as a dull ache filled his mind, like he'd worked out far too hard the day before and was waking to a body riven by lactic acid and overuse.

There was a tug at his jaw and he tasted iodine-laced air. His teeth clenched, no longer biting the bit that had been in his mouth. Seaver coughed and rolled to one side. Something pulled on his arm.

He forced his eyes open and found three black IV lines attached to the crook of his elbow, wrist, and the center of his forearm. His skin…his skin was lime-green. The leads snapped off and a fine blue mist caught him in the face as the lines wriggled up and away.

He groaned a long string of syllables and tried to touch his face, but his fingers bent inward and locked. Seaver tried to pry his digits open, but his other hand locked up. Pain flowed up his bones, like coarse sand had worked its way into each of his joints.

He pulled his body into a fetal position, as each breath became a dull ache in his ribs that grew stronger and stronger with each passing moment.

"Help…" he managed. "Someone…help…"

He felt the press of a cold disc to his neck and

the pain subsided. After a few painful minutes, his limbs and joints loosened and a new, more urgent sensation came to him.

Hunger.

Looking up, he saw a trough full of steaming ground meat in the center of a circular room just beyond a doorway. Seaver rolled off the slab he was on, hit the metal grate of the floor, and crawled toward the food, the smell driving him to an atavistic desire he never knew he could feel.

Using fingerholds in the floor, he pulled himself ahead, ignoring the bloodstains and drains beneath. Numb legs were of little help as he kept moving, like an infant that had just learned to scoot forward.

He got to the trough and shoved a handful of meat into his mouth. It was bland, but Seaver didn't mind. He chomped down, swallowing as fast as he could, choking and hacking up more than once as he ate.

Inez joined him at the feast. The man's skin was also a thin shade of green, his jaw thicker, the bare muscles of his arm and shoulders fuller and better defined than what Seaver remembered.

Seaver gulped down a bite and looked himself over. He'd grown up thin, almost scrawny, but now he had some bulk, a physique of muscle mass built only for the needs of strength and power without an eye to aesthetics. Blood oozed out of injection sites on his arms and legs.

His clavicle itched, and when he went to scratch it, he touched a silver oval. Inez had one in the same place.

Powell clawed her way over the threshold of her room, her eyes wide and locked on the ground-up meat. She was also better built than the last time he'd seen her, her distended jaw making her almost unrecognizable.

Getting to his feet, Seaver went to Powell, grabbing her beneath the arms and dragging her to the trough, where she went in face-first. Seaver squeezed a handful into a ball and popped it into his mouth.

"What…what'd they do to us?" Inez asked as he sank against the trough, one hand on his stomach.

"I don't know." Seaver wiped grease off his

lips. "But I feel taller."

"This shit's awful," Powell said as she chewed, "but I can't stop eating it."

A door slid open and Seaver found himself facing it, not exactly remembering when he turned around.

Legio Keoni was there in full armor, crackling shock maul in hand.

"At ease," he said, his fingers tightening on the maul's handle. "You all still themata. Shaped or no."

"What did you do to us?" Seaver asked. The itch on his silver oval grew stronger, but scratching at it did nothing.

Keoni leveled the maul at him and sidestepped around the wall of the circular room with the trough, not turning his back on the three. He went to a closed door and the seals popped.

"Stay there," Keoni said. "The change still working. You get the maul now, it be bad time for you. For me. Stay."

He pushed the door open and backed into a small room where another person lay on a slab, his body as green and swollen with muscle as Seaver's. The man inside was twitching, his feet jerking back and forth as if in a seizure that would not stop.

Keoni drew a pistol and shot him in the head. The twitching faded away.

"Shape doesn't always catch," Keoni said. "More of you alive than I thought. Good for Lady Juliae. Good for the themata. Albion is good stock, yeah?"

Seaver felt a surge of aggression, the cold splash of adrenaline against his mind. He crouched slightly, on the edge of launching himself at the Daegon servant.

"No!" Keoni swung his pistol up at the hip. "Maintain, boy. Save that for the ferals. Plenty to fight where we're going."

"My face…" Powell ran a hand over her jaw, then down her chest to where her breast tissue had been removed. "What did you do?"

"Shaped you into what Juliae needs," Keoni said. "Clothes in your rooms. Dress now. Juliae has something for you."

"I…need something." Inez stood up, his eyes

drawn. "I was on dust back when I was a kid, got clean, but…I need a fix."

"Body ache now," Keoni said. "More pain in joints coming. Crawlies under the skin next. It only get worse if you wait. Dress. Juliae has your 'fix.'"

Seaver stumbled back to his room and found black fatigues and simple slip-on shoes. He moved quickly and efficiently, the promise of something to take the edge off his pain proved a better motivator than Keoni's maul.

When he came back, he noticed that Keoni— who used to be a half head taller than him—was now a bit shorter. Inez and Powell were in the same black fatigues.

"Lucky, lucky," Keoni said. "Juliae gives you the chance to survive the next fight. Better than rest of the themata. Lucky, lucky. Come." He motioned out the door with his maul.

Seaver was the first through, his eyes locked on the back of Keoni's head as they went through the passageway of the Daegon ship. An inadvertent glance at one of the true Daegon, or any of their thralls with a bit of authority, would mean a beating.

Seaver looked down at his green hands, barely recognizing them. Only a long, thin scar from a childhood hover-bike accident convinced him that he was still in his true body and that his mind hadn't been transferred into something else.

What have they done to me?

Chapter 3

"If I have to say this again, I'm going to scream." Tolan wagged a finger in the air. "We are not going anywhere. Yet."

Loussan, pirate captain of the Harlequin clan, put his hands to his hips and shook his head. Behind him stood a man with short blond hair and a heavy build—Dieter, a Reichsman and mechanic. At the doorway was a scrawny sailor by the name of Geet, who looked like he wanted to be anywhere but there.

"The longer we stay," Loussan said, "the more danger we're in. The Daegon will realize who *you* are, what this ship really is, and then, by Caishen, we'll be in an even worse situation. If that's even possible. We can slip away."

Tolan, sitting in one of two seats on the cramped bridge of the *Joaquim*, waved a hand toward the front windows where Daegon warships loomed large just outside Bucky Station over Concord. A steady stream of fighters and cargo ships drifted from the armada toward the planet and back.

"Oh, I'm sorry, do my eyes deceive me?" Tolan asked. "Because it looks like we could almost walk across Daegon hulls from here to the slip-space point."

"We have a stealth drive!" Loussan said, tossing his hands up.

"But does it even work?" Tolan raised an eyebrow at Dieter.

"I have to run the power drives through the system to calibrate everything," Dieter said, looking to one side. "And I can't do that until we're under way."

"And if we try to leave this space dock, the Daegon will blow us into smithereens—maybe down to reens. Or smithers," Tolan said. "So no stealth drive. And stop thinking I've got my ship sitting here because I like the view."

"There has to be a hack to the stealth drive," Loussan said, putting a hand on Dieter's shoulder. The Reichsman looked at the hand, then at the pirate. "You're the tech expert. Just...tweak it. Help us get out of here."

Dieter brushed Loussan's hand away. "This is precision Reich tech," Dieter said. "This isn't some fifth-generation Cathay garbage that you bought at some flea market. The Reich has standards when it creates technology, and I will not bastardize such a beautiful piece of machinery."

"So you could do it...if you wanted to?" Loussan rubbed his hands together.

"And the explosion from one misaligned *Unterbrochener Stromkreislauf* will take out half this station," Dieter said. "The testing facility on Dallas Secundus used to be much larger. I heard."

"If you did your Reich-y best," Tolan said, "what chance would you give us to undock and engage the stealth field before the Daegon—or a tech oopsie—blows us up?"

Dieter looked up and mumbled to himself, "Three percent...of us not exploding. Less if the

Daegon have us dialed in and shoot us in the ninety seconds it takes to bring everything online." Dieter frowned.

"So you're saying there's a chance." Loussan smiled.

"No. There's no chance." Tolan slapped his thighs. "Squat and hold. Hurry up and wait. Take both thumbs and proceed to sit on them as best you can. But that doesn't mean we can't be proactive."

"And do what?" Dieter asked. "Daegon soldiers are patrolling the docks. If we even open a hatch, they'll shoot us down. We all saw what they did to the freighter in the next slip."

"We can take care of a few Daegon," Loussan said. "Let me get Ruprecht out of his box and he can—"

"Ah ah!" Tolan brandished an index finger. "There's no box."

"What box?" Dieter asked.

"There is a box." Loussan nodded slowly.

"Forget about the box," Tolan said through gritted teeth.

"I have my Katar in hibernation," Loussan

said to the Reichsman. "In a box. That is real."

"That was need-to-know information." Tolan touched his face and pulled one cheek back. "And the wrench monkey didn't need to know that."

"A…Katar?" Dieter backed away from Loussan toward the other seat. "One of those nightmare cyborgs is on this ship?"

"He's very well-behaved for a cyborg assassin," Loussan said. "Only kills people when I tell him to. Tells the best dick and fart jokes too, once you get to know him."

"You can't have one of those things here," Dieter said. "If it gets loose, then…then…"

"It'll be a problem for the Daegon…and us, once they trace him back," Tolan said. "I doubt it'll be as simple as 'Does this anthropomorphic blender belong to you?' and we try to 'whoopsie' our way out of it. He stays in the box."

"I hate all this waiting," Loussan said, pacing back and forth. The few steps it took to cross the bridge and his exaggerated turns made Tolan roll his eyes.

"Then we need to—ah! There…" Tolan

24

pointed to one side as a cargo ship unmoored and flew slowly toward a Daegon ship. "See…told you the Daegon didn't blow us all up for no reason at all. They need us for…something."

"They've invaded star systems from Albion into Cathay," Dieter said. "You think they're going to need this rust bucket?"

"I'd be offended, but I really need your services right now," Tolan said. "If we wait for the Daegon to need us, then…"

"I can calibrate the stealth drive properly," Dieter said.

"And Ruprecht can deal with any problem we have aboard." Loussan narrowed his eyes.

"Geet, finish this thought problem," Tolan said and the three men turned to the pirate in the back.

"I have soup on the stove," Geet said. "It's potato and I found some dried herbs in the galley. Can I go take a glance at it? Check the seasoning?"

"Then we can be on our merry way back to Albion." Tolan buried his hands in his face. "Thanks for playing, Geet. Real value-added right there. Go, go. Get lunch."

Geet pressed his hands together in thanks and scurried away.

"Wrench monkey, have you ever had to get through a customs inspection?" Tolan asked.

"You keep calling me that like it's an insult," Dieter said. "Yes, I've gone through customs before."

"Have you gone through whilst your ship is full of contraband and one wrong word will land you in prison?" Tolan asked.

"Well...not exactly."

"Then it's time to play a little game called 'Get our stories straight,'" Tolan said. "Loussan, you know this one?"

"I'm a freebooter." Loussan turned his nose up. "I wasn't one to submit to some jackboot telling me what I could bring in and out of a star system."

"Especially when you probably stole it." Tolan ran a hand through his hair. "Amateurs, the both of you. Geet has plenty of experience playing dumb; you two have to learn your parts. So, first things first. The name of this ship is..."

Chapter 4

Thorvald walked down a passageway to where Salis, his fellow Genevan bodyguard, stood outside a quarter's door. His armor's AI reached out to hers and the two suits exchanged data.

After checking quickly behind him to ensure they were alone, his helmet split open along the T-line on his visor and retracted to the back of his head.

Salis' helmet did the same.

"How is it?" she asked.

"The Kongs will let us talk. That's progress," he said.

"Any progress with Grynau?" she asked, naming the AI within his armor.

"He's still fighting me. Yours?"

She sucked air through her teeth and shook her head.

"They told me our AI would have blocks when I was at our House," she said, "but nothing like this. Why won't they let us tell Gage that he's King Randolph's son?" She cocked her head to one side, then raised her voice to say, "Why won't they let us—ah!" She grimaced as the armor tightened around her throat.

"That happens every time I try to tell Gage." Thorvald shook his head. "I was there when the Kongs challenged his authority as regent. The AI should know enough to help us help our principals."

"You wear the old captain's armor," she said. "His AI was privy to files restricted by the King. Are they still blacked out?"

"I am not the captain," Thorvald said, "no matter what I do to prove myself to Gage or the AI...the captain's armor possessed the succession list. That's why it favored Gage over Lady Christina at New Madras. The AI accepted Gage as regent originally because of his rank and Prince' Aidan's age..."

"This isn't hard to piece together anymore," Salis said, shaking her head. "Gage is on the true succession list maintained in our armor, but he's there because he's the King's son, not only because of his rank. But our AI won't let us tell him the truth."

"The AI are focused on protecting Gage and Aidan, and maintaining the integrity of files blacked out to us is consistent with their programming," Thorvald said. "Frustrating. Nearly twenty years in the service of House Ticino and I've never experienced this before."

"Given how you acquired your armor and AI…"

"Yes…" Thorvald looked away. "Yes, I tore this suit off Captain Royce's body so I could save the royal family. And there have been issues ever since. The AI functions as designed during routine duties, but I can't access everything in the database."

"And I never swore my oaths to the King properly so my access is limited." Salis rolled her eyes. "Our House designed the AI to be impossible to hack, yet here we are held back by our own safeguards."

"There is a solution," Thorvald said.

"No, don't even suggest it." She shook her head.

"Gage needs to know the truth."

"Does he?" Salis' voice raised slightly. "Gage learns he's the bastard son of King Randolph and then what? He can't be regent any more than he already is by right of his rank."

"Albion succession isn't that strict." Thorvald touched the side of his helmet. "The King can designate whoever he wants as his successor. Randolph may have put Gage higher than Aidan. Gage is of the bloodline. That's the only hard-and-fast rule."

Salis flopped her arms up in frustration. "And we don't have access to the list because of the AI's blocks, but what does it matter if Gage is the true King right now?"

"If he's King, then he's in a better position to make treaties with the League. Albion's sovereign is just a boy right now, with Gage acting on his behalf. There's no guarantee Aidan will keep to Gage's promises once he's of age," Thorvald said.

"You're putting too much thought into all this," she sniffed. "Our oath is to keep them safe, not grease their political skids."

"Gage as King will have an easier time with the rest of the League," Thorvald said. "I spent almost two decades in the royal palace. Hard not to learn the rules of the grand game—things they don't teach back at the Academy."

"Too many what if's," she said. "And we can't tell any of this to Gage without our AI stopping us."

"Then we take off the armor," Thorvald said.

Salis looked him in the eyes and shook her head. "No, Thorvald. We do that and the AI will never accept us again. We can't protect them without this," she said, putting a palm to her breastplate.

"We swore to our last dying breath to Albion," he said. "Nothing in that oath requires us to be suited."

"Without the armor, we're no better than any of the armed sailors on guard through this ship—ugh, my AI's going into conniptions just because we're discussing this. Stop before the bonds degrade anymore."

"It's the right thing to do," Thorvald said.

"How? You tell Gage, then *maybe* he gets a leg up in negotiations? Put yourself in the Kong's or the Reich's place. Commodore Gage suddenly announces he's the King of Albion so long after the invasion and the death of Randolph. Think, Thorvald, how will the other great powers take that news?"

Thorvald frowned. "Gage is a pretender and an opportunist...particularly after he sidelined Lady Christina back on New Madras."

"Exactly. And you'll have given up your armor and your best means to protect Gage for nothing...even if Gage believes you," she said.

"The star nations will believe he's the King...if only we can access all the files our AI have blacked out." Thorvald took a deep breath.

"And we're pretty far from Geneva and our House artificers to get that access," she said. "Forget it. We do the best we can with what we have and keep to our oath."

"Perhaps we get Dr. Seaver to do a DNA match and—" Thorvald grimaced as his armor briefly tightened around his neck and throat.

"We can't share medical information," she said. "Makes it too easy for a threat to craft a gene-specific poison."

"Then what are we supposed to do?" Thorvald asked.

"Hold the line." Salis' shoulders drooped. "There's no perfect solution to any of this. We risk too much for too little gain to tell Gage what we know. Just hold the line."

The door to Aidan's quarters opened and the Genevans' armor snapped back over their faces.

Bertram, still pale and sickly-looking from his near drowning on New Madras, rubbed an eye. "I say, don't you two ever sleep?" he asked.

"No," Thorvald deadpanned.

"Well, young master Aidan will be up soon and he likes his eggs cooked just so," Bertram said. "Coming in? I can make a few extra if you like."

"I will accompany the regent to Lantau shortly," Thorvald said.

"Then why are you here? Shouldn't you be off intimidating the shuttle crew to have every nut and bolt screwed down tighter?" Bertram asked. "But if you're going to the surface, perhaps you can pick up some spices for the kitchen…"

Thorvald put a finger to Bertram's chest and pushed him back into the Prince's quarters.

"Don't let Gage get stabbed down there," Salis said.

"A minor flesh wound is the least of my worries," Thorvald said. "The Kongs can be worse than pirates."

Chapter 5

Robot arms pressed a breastplate to Seaver's chest, the thin chain-mail body glove pinching against his skin as a servo whirled and then locked into the rest of Seaver's armor. He stood spread-eagle, gripping a ring as more robot arms fixed plates to him.

The pain of the grafts didn't bother him…in fact, he was starting to like it.

Across the armory, row upon row of Daegon soldiers stepped into the rings and servo arms fixed their panoply to their bodies.

Juliae walked in front of Seaver, her helmet in the crook of an arm, the light of a holo projection on contact lenses playing out across her eyes. She was rarely seen without her helmet donned, and Seaver got his first good look at her.

She appeared young, barely into her twenties, with short black hair worn slicked back, ending just below her jawline. Emerald eyes stood in contrast to the deep purple of her skin.

Despite being one of the Daegon that wrecked his home world and forced him into being a slave soldier, he was taken by her good looks.

"Seaver," she said, holding up a small metal vial. "You have been reshaped by the Daegon to serve us better."

As she spoke, Seaver first heard the Daegon language, slightly muted, then her words played over his hearing in English.

"I serve." Seaver spoke in English, but he said, *"Ego serviam,"* and the words tasted like ashes.

"Your implanted translator is working. Good. You will not offend your master's ears with feral language. If you are found wanting, your family will pay the price with you…a father in need of medical treatment for Langfei Syndrome. Your body is stronger, faster, elevated from your pathetic state as a themata, but this gift comes with conditions.

"As one that's been shaped, you are to be my personal guard and attendant. Keoni and the other legio must keep the themata in line. You and the others are to keep the enemy from disturbing me during combat. This…" She reached up and snapped the vial to the top of his breastplate. There was a buzz as the plate snapped the vial beneath the armor and a cool sensation washed over Seaver's body. "This is my DNA key. Without it, your body will reject the shaping and you will die in agony in short order. You felt the bone curse after you were awakened. You'll go through much worse without my DNA key. I die…you die. Then your father will pay for your failure. This is understood?"

"Yes, Lady Juliae," Seaver said.

She touched a sigil of a clenched fist on her breastplate. "The Daegon, who rule all of humanity," she said, moving a fingertip to a smaller circle bearing a sphinx to one side of the fist. "House Asaria, for whose glory we fight."

She touched a golden circle of a snake consuming its own tail beneath the sphinx. "Lord

Eubulus, our liege." Then a starburst slightly smaller than the Ouroboros beneath that—all three crests were to the same side of the fist sigil—and she beat a fist to one shoulder and clicked her heels together.

"Nicias. Our commander," she said. "You fail me and you have failed them all. Serve well and you will be rewarded."

"Yes, Lady Juliae," Seaver felt a vibration through the arming ring and he stepped down. Even in his flesh-wrought body, he still wasn't as tall as the Daegon woman. "I…want a weapon." He flexed his hands open and shut.

"When we make the assault," she said, pressing her lips slightly and narrowing her eyes for a moment. "Concord. Tell me of this planet."

"Concord…second expansion world. Settled by an old Earth people from Finland, I think. Finland and New England. Very independent. They never signed any mutual defense treaties. I remember something from when I was a kid about them…my mother was on a hospital ship and had to make an emergency stop at their station. She couldn't go on shore leave in her uniform—the locals would've given her trouble. When she came back to her shuttle, someone had sprayed graffiti on the hull. 'Live free or die.' Something like that."

"Those words…they truly mean them?" Juliae asked.

"During the last big war, the Reich was conquering systems all through that part of space…but they never attacked Concord. Rumor was that the Concord prime minister took a Reich envoy on a tour of a small city, and every man, woman, and child that could hold a rifle was there, all armed. Reich bypassed the system."

Juliae mumbled under her breath.

"The initial attack on Concord has stalled," she said. "The planet did not surrender after our fleet secured their orbit. Lord Nicias opted for an orbital assault to quell the populace and encountered a more…tenacious resistance. Each Daegon officer was allotted shaped themata to better protect us on the ground. It seems these Concordians have a knack for finding and killing leadership targets."

"Concord…has a reputation," Seaver said.

"And once we rip their heart out, the rest of

feral space will know we cannot be beaten, no matter how fanatical the resistance. The Baroness has already brought Albion into compliance. Lord Eubulus fights over New Madras. Now Nicias will teach Concord that they will be ruled. *Novis Regiray.*"

"Novis Regiray," Seaver said, and a bit of calm pulsed out of the DNA lock in his chest armor.

Juliae cocked her head slightly. "Nicias has final orders for us. Come, you may have something useful to add." She reached down and picked up a helmet from the arming station and tossed it to Seaver. The skull motif of the faceplate was scuffed, a bullet-sized patch on one side. Seaver put it on…and smelled old blood.

****

Seaver, Powell, and Inez followed Juliae through a gap between massed ranks of themata soldiers. The cavern of the *Sitheno*'s main landing bay was oddly silent, given the presence of thousands of soldiers. The low whine of idling shuttle engines and the tap of the Daegon's boots were all Seaver could hear through his helmet.

He carried an assault rifle with a boxed ammunition magazine, links of high-caliber bullets with red tips feeding into the breach, and more magazines loaded onto his back. The weapon would have needed a crew of three to emplace and fire properly, but his armor and enhanced physique made it easy to carry. A bayonet with a serrated blade was in a thigh scabbard.

The themata wore simple dark fatigues with flak vests and helmets that left their faces visible. Each had a simple rifle slung over their shoulders and a kit with canteens, ammunition and a single medical pouch in web gear over their shoulders and around their waists. Men and women stretched their necks against the touch of the silver torques, none daring to break discipline and scratch at them.

Seaver almost missed a step as he realized his own torque was gone. The thought of dying slowly and painfully from withdrawal almost seemed worse than the quick death the torques promised when they constricted on the Daegon's command and severed arteries.

Their eyes wide, the slave soldiers had fear written on their faces, and more than one was panting. Seaver wasn't sure who had the worse situation. When they died, their ordeal was done. If he failed in his duty to keep Juliae alive, his father would pay the ultimate price. Juliae, at least, was interested in living. None of the Daegon seemed to care if the themata lived another day.

Keoni reversed the grip on his shock maul and saluted Juliae with a fist across his chest. "Eighty-seven at your command," he said, his words sounding in Seaver's ears through linked radio.

"It was ninety-one this morning." She drew a pistol from a holster and slapped a magazine battery into the grip.

"Three attempted self-death," Keoni said. "One succeeded. Two stabilized and sent to the golems. They die…but they die again. Last refused to leave the barracks. *Sitheno* crew claimed her and took her to the pits."

"Names…I'll see the kill orders sent on to Albion. Play the execution videos once they catch up to us. Those that survive this planet will have a better understanding of their duties," she said. "They die by my command and their families survive. Any other death is unacceptable."

"Yes, master," Keoni said. "We depart soon? Themata think too much before a fight…no good."

"The assault begins when it begins." She touched a forearm and tapped on a screen. A breath of cool air seemed to pass over Seaver's body from the vial attached to his clavicle, and his knees almost buckled.

"Tranqs?" Keoni said, his voice hazy.

"I'll hit them with the rage once we're near," she said.

The air over the waiting shuttles crackled and a massive hologram formed. A Daegon with a widow's peak and sharp nose turned to the camera, and Seaver was dragged down to one knee by an impulse he'd never felt before. He heard the shuffle of thousands of others as the themata made their obedience known. Only Juliae and other Daegon officers remained standing.

"Ground regiments, this is Lord Nicias," boomed from the holo. "Code havoc in effect. No prisoners. No mercy. I want all the ferals dead by sunrise or you will answer to me." The holo scrambled and vanished.

"Themata Three-Seven Omicron, embark!" Juliae waved the hand gripping her pistol forward and her soldiers marched into the wide mouth of a waiting transport ship and onto rows of canvas crash seats outfitted with crude straps.

The soldiers seated themselves, few daring to look at Juliae, but Seaver caught more than one pair of eyes lingering on him and the other two shaped.

Juliae, Keoni, and her escort went up the ramp. Keoni took a seat in the front, laying his shock maul across his lap as he strapped in. The rest went to the back of the hold, where Juliae put her back to a bulkhead and belts crisscrossed over her body, securing her far better than her soldiers. She motioned to the bulkhead next to her and Seaver mimicked her stance. Clamps bit against his boots and a force pushed him back against the bulkhead.

"Mag locks," she said. "Keep your grip on your rifle…we're landing in Daegon territory. Should be uneventful. From there, we join the assault on their capitol building. A place called the Hexen."

"You are most kind to share with us," Inez said. "Thank you."

Seaver was glad his helmet covered his face, hiding from Juliae the look of disgust he gave to Inez.

"Mind your tongue," Juliae said. "You don't need it to be shaped. If I shed blood on this planet, all of you will get a lash for each drop."

The ramp raised with a pneumatic whine and slammed shut, plunging the troop hold into darkness. Weak red lights lit up along the bulkheads.

Juliae removed her helmet and ran fingers through her hair. She stared at something on the inside of her visor, and for the first time, Seaver saw a flicker of emotion cross her face. She huffed and put her helm back on.

Maybe she's human after all, he thought.

The shuttle's engines rumbled as they came to power, and with a lurch, they took off.

Seaver heard several prayers from the themata, and Keoni did nothing to stop them. There was a grip on his wrist. Powell had taken a hand off her machine gun and was clutching him. Seaver moved his hand up and held hers. Even beneath her skull mask, he could tell she was afraid…and so was he. The emotion was there, buried deep beneath whatever drug Juliae had hit him with, waiting to grow and get loose into his mind.

He thought of his father, who should be at his regular bocce ball game with the other retirees—if the Daegon still allowed any sort of freedom to those they conquered. What would his father think of him now? Was he a traitor for bearing arms in the enemy's service, or a loving son that sacrificed so that his father might live?

And his mother…he had no idea. The Daegon said she was dead, and if the *Orion* was destroyed, then she must be. She always harped on the virtues of nonviolence, that healing the wounded was far better than being the one that wounds…and look at him now.

He pulled his hand away from Powell's and held his weapon firmly, glancing at Juliae. The lenses of her visor snapped with images and information.

There was no easy way out of this, he realized. All he could do was survive.

Chapter 6

The *Sphinx* was a city in and of itself. A dome covered the miles and miles of densely packed facilities over the anti-grav engines and hangar bays built into the bottom layer of the structure. It loomed over New Exeter, a metropolis of nearly twenty million souls, like a mail fist about to strike.

At the apex, only a few hundred meters from the dome, Baroness Asaria held court. Gilded in gold and platinum, her throne was the only fixture that sat on a bloodred carpet of silk woven through with images of angels battling serpents. Rings of humans in bondage, forever following the slave in front of them, radiated out from the throne at the center.

Asaria paced back and forth before her throne, the metal of her armor coiling up and down her limbs like a snake.

Gustavus knelt before her, his fists planted against the rug, his sword drawn and laid out before him. Tiberian stood behind and to one side, hands clasped behind him.

Daegon officers stood along the perimeter, silent as they watched Asaria continue to pace. Four cloaked men and women waited behind the throne, data feeds shining off their flat visors, oversized headsets buzzing with static and an overlay of muted voices.

"And your father, Lord Eubulus, died in battle with the Reich?" Asaria asked. Her voice was stern, not a match for the anger behind her eyes.

"They attacked without warning or provocation, Master," Gustavus said, not daring to lift his gaze from the floor. "We had the battle won. The Indus were breaking. The feral Albion ships were in our grasp and—"

Asaria reached back and struck at Gustavus. Her living armor uncoiled and barbs snapped out of the iron-gray metal as it wrapped around Gustavus' face and neck. He froze as electricity ripped down the length of the metal and into his body, a dull scream sounding through his clenched jaw.

"This is true?" Asaria asked Tiberian, her eyes locked on the younger commander suffering under her lash.

"I was planet-side when the Reich attacked," Tiberian said. "I reviewed my ship's logs. The whelp speaks the truth."

Asaria pulled her arm back and the armor retracted, forming a *manica* armguard.

Gustavus collapsed to his elbows for a moment, then pushed himself back to his hands and knees. Blood dripped from his lips and struck a gold-plated box dangling from a chain around his neck.

"Three battleships lost at New Madras," Asaria said. "The rest of the assault force retreated under your command," she said to Tiberian.

"That ship of theirs, the *Castle Itter,*" Tiberian said shaking his head, "she changed the battle calculus. To continue that fight risked a total loss."

"Eubulus was wrong to trust the Reich." Asaria picked up Gustavus' sword and ran a fingertip down the blade, coating the edge with her blood. She watched as the cut healed right before her eyes. "All that effort we put into subverting the Kaiserina, into convincing her that she was worthy to rule alongside the Daegon once we brought the ferals back under our yoke…" She snapped the blade out at one of the officers along the edge of the throne room.

"Cleon…your specters are still in Reich territory. What are they reporting?" she asked.

"The Reich remains neutral, publicly, master," the officer said. "My operatives say that word of the battle at New Madras hasn't reached the Kaiserina, and their military has yet to fully mobilize…it is possible the *Castle Itter* acted of its own accord."

"An Unter-Duke by the name of Klaven was in command," Tiberian said. "Young…stupid."

"Show me the war," she said to the four behind her throne. They looked up as one and a holo field projected off their faces, forming a disc just above their heads and coalescing into a local galactic map.

"Our advance through Cathay space continues," Asaria said as red lines extended away from Albion and deep into other star nations' territory. "The Indus managed to stop us at New Madras, but other armadas seized Kolkata and Guwahati…the Indus can't even reinforce New Madras since we took the nearest slip systems."

"The Cathay refuse to allow other nations to transit their territory," Cleon said. "The Golden Emperor is frozen with indecision. He's not convinced the League is the answer to our return. As we anticipated," the spymaster added with a smile.

"The fall of New Madras would have sent the Indus groveling to us." Asaria put the blade against Gustavus' bare neck. "Now it has turned into a rallying cry against us. The ferals have a victory."

Gustavus raised his head slightly, giving her an easier strike to end his life.

"You carry your father's writ," Asaria said, "but you are not Eubulus. You are just a child."

"Let me go back," Gustavus said. "I will burn the planet and—"

Asaria flicked the sword and the writ fell to the floor, the chain severed.

"You are not your father." She stabbed the tip into the floor. "You can be trained to replace him.

You will not repeat his mistakes, will you?"

"No, Master," Gustavus said.

"Unless you believe he would fail at command," Asaria asked, raising an eyebrow at Tiberian. "Would you keep him on as one of your hunters?"

"He wants blood," Tiberian said. "Let him have his fill."

"Assign him a cruiser and integrate his command into the *classis* fleet we're building now." She pointed to another officer along the perimeter. "Rise, Gustavus. Return to me in victory or I'll send you to the golems."

Using the sword poking out of the ground to get to his feet, Gustavus pried it out, saluted the Baroness with it, then went to an empty spot along the edge.

"We are overextended," Asaria said, raising a hand to the holo above them all. "Our fleets have reached the limits of our ability to supply them, but we have achieved what the other Houses demanded of us for our great reconquest: the ferals are in chaos. They have not united against us, and we must keep them disorganized until the rest of the Daegon arrive to join us in this war."

"We don't need them," an officer said. "The ferals are just as weak as ever. They have no knowledge of our true strength. Make the push for Earth and they will collapse. They will beg us to be their lords instead of being destroyed."

"How many years have we planned for this?" Asaria asked, walking around the circle of officers. "For centuries, we've watched the ferals from beyond the Veil. Generations of spies infiltrating their governments and military. The plan was prepared, agreed to by all the High Houses, and our House was given the finest resources with the writ to prepare the way for the rest of the Daegon. We are to strike the blow that will shatter the feral's resolve…and we have yet to succeed."

She went to Tiberian and plucked the writ off the chain around his neck. When she pressed a sharp thumbnail against the box, a holo capture from his armor played out around the throne.

Salis, clutching Prince Aidan at her side, backed away toward the edge of a broken bridge. A portly man with a pistol stepped between the boy and Tiberian.

"You cannot have him!" Salis cried and jumped into an icy river, taking the boy prince and the man with her.

"Dead?" Asaria asked.

"Dead," Tiberian said. "We recovered the male and he confirmed. Another of the Genevans intervened while I interrogated. If the boy was alive, the other Genevan wouldn't have bothered with the servant."

"Broadcast the footage but digitally create the boy's corpse," Asaria said. "Evaluate local sentiment after that."

"This world is in compliance," Cleon said. "My inquisitors—"

"Yet the free Albion ships remain a problem," Asaria said. "They rallied the Indus. They fought at New Madras. Now they go to Lantau to join the ferals under one banner." She squeezed Tiberian's writ in her fist and the box melted and reincorporated into her armor.

"The Oculus is nearly open," Asaria said.

"The next phase of our return to humanity…one we cannot jeopardize. The High Houses will arrive here and find a planet under our yoke and the path laid out for them to seize their own domains. Victory is nearly here."

"And the gathering at Lantau?" Tiberian asked.

"Cleon?" Asaria half turned to the spymaster.

"It will fail," the spymaster said. "Our asset is in place."

"Hope is our foe," Asaria said, "but it can also be a lure. Let's bait a trap, yes? Bring me a plan tomorrow morning. Dismissed."

Tiberian bowed at the waist and turned to leave, when he felt a slight tug at his wrist.

A willow branch of her armor slithered back up her arm and she looked at him with a gleam in her eye, bidding him to come closer.

He waited for the rest of the others to leave down a concentric stairwell surrounding the throne dais. Then he took her hand and sat in the throne. She snuggled onto his lap and they embraced as the ornate seat sank into the floor.

Chapter 7

The Reich shuttle jittered through turbulence as it flew through Lantau's atmosphere. Klaven leaned forward slightly in his seat and looked out a porthole to a diffuse orange glow emanating up from beneath the cloud layer.

"I've heard some…fascinating things about Cathay cities," Klaven said to Gage and Birbal. Both men sat on the same row of seats, each in full-dress uniforms. Gage held a sword across his lap, his red tunic laden with medals, a green crown on his epaulets denoting his rank as regent. Birbal wore an alabaster-white uniform with a turban embossed with a gold badge the size of his palm.

"Population densities higher than any other

planet in settled space," Klaven continued. "Arcologies where the residents spend their entire lives and never see the sky…"

"The Cathay settled star systems with few earthlike planets," Birbal said. "They're used to tight quarters of dome cities on moons and orbital stations. Or maybe they just like living on top of each other."

"I've heard—strictly rumor, naturally—that the Cathay have plenty of living space. It's just that the Emperor charges so much for land that his people would rather live like ants than pay up. Look down there—we've been flying over a metropolis for nearly half an hour. How many people are there?"

"Beijing on Old Earth was larger than many European countries before the Mount Edziza Eruption," Birbal said with a shrug.

"Gentlemen," Gage said, "can we get back to the matter at hand?"

"Oh, we're in solidarity with you, Commodore," Klaven said. "That's why I insisted we all take my shuttle. Show the League that I and the Indus have full confidence in Albion."

"You said 'I' and not 'the Reich,'" Gage said,

looking at the younger commander.

"Yes, that's true." Klaven shifted in his seat. "I'm not authorized to speak for Kaiserina Washington, as my poor deceased minder Diaz would have piped up with by now. Lord bless his soul."

"I do not believe the League will be especially pleased to see a Reich battleship in orbit," Birbal said. "No offense to you, Unter-Duke."

"The League was formed as a block to the Reich's colonial expansion." Klaven waved a hand in front of his face. "I'm well aware. But now we have the Daegon to deal with and, as the Kongs say, *'kapshi kapshida.'* We all go forward together, yes?"

"That's Korean," Gage said. "And I'm guessing you learned that phrase from Busan…a Cathay world the Reich conquered during your last 'colonial expansion.'"

"Rapoto," Klaven said, looking around the side of his seat to his Genevan bodyguard, "remind me not to say that phrase in front of the Kongs."

"I am not your babysitter," the Genevan said.

"It will keep them from getting angry with me and that means less work for you." Klaven wagged a finger at the man and turned back to Gage.

"The Daegon are the issue," Birbal said. "With their attack on League worlds, a declaration of war should be easy to obtain…if they haven't made one already."

"I can promise the Reich's neutrality," Klaven said. "At the very least. For now. Kaiserina Washington isn't interested in another full-scale war. That was made clear to me before the *Castle Itter* and I set off for our cruise."

"Because there are a half-dozen active rebellions on Reich worlds," Gage said.

"Commodore, I would be more annoyed with you if you weren't always so correct," Klaven said.

"The League doesn't appreciate diplomatic language during a crisis," Birbal said. "I was an intern at Manchukuo during the last Mechanix incursion. Saw the Cathay go through three different ambassadors before the Emperor got one that said what he actually wanted."

"What happened to the other two?" Klaven asked.

Birbal ran a finger across his throat.

"That's the Cathay for you," the Reichsman said with a sigh.

"And the Daegon are…one of several elephants in the room," Birbal said, looking at Gage. "Your honor and courage will be made known to the League, Commodore. None will dispute it."

"But they will demand an explanation from me as to why Albion ships are fighting beside the Daegon," Gage said. "That's my elephant."

"If it had a color, I'm sure it would be white," Klaven said. "Do your people play that game around *erste feiertag*? Boxing Day, you might call it? Christmas? Diwali?"

"Thank you, Klaven," Gage said, the bay lights going red as the shuttle neared the landing pad. "If more Reichsmen were like you, we wouldn't need a League."

"I daresay the situation would be even worse right now without the League," Klaven said. "Though I am the first of the Reich to attend such a function since… Reuilly."

"And that meeting was bombed," Birbal said.

"A bombing the Reich had nothing to do

with," Klaven added quickly. "We wanted the Second Reach War to end too."

The shuttle landed with a whine of engines and both Thorvald and Rapoto made their way down the ramp before it could lower completely.

The sound and smell of rain wafted into the shuttle as Gage unbuckled and straightened his tunic. Birbal and Klaven had attendants spruce up their uniforms as Gage made his way to the top of the ramp. Alone.

Beyond the ramp was a diffuse glow through rain and fog from either side of the shuttle. The landing pad extended to an ash-colored haze leading away from the ramp. The two Genevans stood at the ready at either corner of the ramp, carbines in hand. A steady rhythm of heavy footfalls sounded in the gloom, growing louder with each step. The rustle of chains and whine of servos came with it.

Rainwater dripped off the aft of the shuttle in thin columns.

"Ugh, weather," Klaven said, putting on a rounded helmet with the Reich crest and a feathered top. He tightened a glossy black chin strap and clicked silver spurs together before he and the Indus commander joined Gage at the top of the ramp.

"I'm sure they ordered it just for you," Birbal said. "I'm just glad it's not cold here."

Out of the fog came two columns of Cathay soldiers—tall Cathay soldiers. Each man stood nearly seven feet with a horsehair tassel at the top of the helmets that displayed close-cropped, bearded faces and came down past the chin line. Each carried a dao sword, both hands gripping the hilt and holding the blade straight down ahead of them, the pommel at their waist. The soldiers wore chain mail of bronze and silver that rattled with each step.

The rain stopped as they neared, but only over the soldiers. Gage still heard it falling on the shuttle top.

Four robots carried an ornate palanquin out of the thick fog. The box mounted onto two poles was solid gold, with dragon motifs worked into every inch of the surface, the end of each pole a snarling head of the creatures of legend.

The robots turned the side of the palanquin toward the ramp, their movements synchronized and perfect as only machines could manage. They set the box down gently and the door opened with a hiss of escaping air.

An elderly Cathay man in long white robes trimmed in deep-blue got out, his hands stuffed into overly wide sleeves, his lengthy goatee—the hair so thin, it was nearly a wisp—fluttering in the breeze. A tall black cap covered the top of his head.

"Which one of you is the asshole?" the man asked, shuffling forward and squinting at the three officers.

Klaven pointed at his chest, then to Gage, confusion writ across his face, his fingertip switching back and forth between him and the regent.

"I know you're an asshole, Reichsman," the old man said. "I can tell who you are by your ridiculous hat. No question about that. My eyes are bad and I can't tell which of the others is the jackboot…"

"Commodore Thomas Gage," he said, stepping off the ramp and extending a hand to the Cathay official. "HMS *Orion*. 11th Fleet. Commanding."

"Shin," said the old man, removing a liver-spotted hand from his robes. The pinky nail was long and inlaid with gold. He held his hand out limply for Gage to shake. "Counselor Shin. I represent the Emperor on Lantau."

"Your hospitality is appreciated—" Klaven began.

"Shut it." Shin waved him off. "You Reich nobles have a reputation of vowing to conquer any planet you step foot on. Promise me you're not that stupid. You've got one oversized target of a ship in orbit and that's all."

"A horrid rumor spread by the Reich's enemies." Klaven put a hand to his chest and lifted a foot to walk off the ramp.

"Eh!" Shin wagged a finger at him.

"The Reich has no territorial claim to Lantau and my presence is strictly diplomatic," Klaven said with a roll of his eyes.

"Fine, fine," Shin said, waving Birbal over. "Never any worries with this kind of Indus—so long as you don't touch any of that fabric wrapped around their head," the old man cackled.

Birbal, one hand resting on the hilt of a sword, smiled slightly.

"Are we to discuss matters here?" Gage looked up at a force field overhead as rain spattered against it.

"At least you don't want to waste my time," Shin said, shuffling back to his litter. "I've got the antechamber ready for you all. The sooner I can get the Albion off the planet, the better. If the peasants find out he's here, the riots will get even worse."

"Not the palace?" Klaven asked as the three men followed slowly behind Shin.

"Heh." Shin waved a hand dismissively. "The palace is only for the Emperor, and he's very particular about who gets inside. I've got labor bots sprucing the place up now, robots that should be building bunkers and such, but nooooo…our most glorious Emperor wants the flower patterns in the gardens and the artwork to match the season on the Forbidden Continent. Has to be perfect before his arrival or he'll toss my old bones out onto the street."

"The Emperor is coming here?" Gage asked.

"Yes." Shin pointed a clawed hand at him.

"And that's a problem for you, Albion. A serious problem. He's contemplating just how to respond to your treachery. I was discussing with General Han on how we should've dealt with you the second you came out of slip space. But the Reich and the Indus got in the way. I've got some latitude here, but not that much."

"Albion stands with the League," Gage said. "I don't understand why those—"

"Save it." Shin flopped back into the litter and shook out the hem of his robes. "League reps are in the antechamber ready and waiting to hear you out. We'll put you to a committee vote."

He pulled the door shut and the robots lifted him up and took him away.

"Keep up," Shin called out from inside, "unless you want to get wet." He cackled as the soldiers escorting him turned around and followed.

Gage and the other officers fell back a few paces, staying just within the edge of the force-field umbrella overhead.

Around them, skyscrapers decked out in flashing neon signs with Cathay language shone through the fog like beacons. Lights from passing air cars and drones formed lanes in the sky, all keeping a distance from the airfield and low lights of the palace ahead of them.

"That could have gone better," Birbal said. "At least they're willing to talk."

"You're quite the hot button, Gage," Klaven said. "Can't imagine why."

"Albion and Cathay have been allies for centuries," Gage said. "Never an armed dispute between our people…now they think we're on the side of the Daegon."

"Nice not being the most hated guy in the room," Klaven said and Birbal gave him a dirty look. "What? The Reich hasn't exactly been welcome in the League for quite some time. Not that League ships have been in the New Prussia or Odessa systems either. Let's consider this a bit of progress, yes?"

"No matter what the League reps decide," Birbal said to Gage, "you're welcome with the Indus."

"Thank you." Gage glanced back and saw Thorvald just behind him. "Tell the truth, I'd rather be back on my bridge getting ready to fight the

Daegon than dealing with this...diplomatic issue."

"You'll be fine." Klaven gave him a pat on the back. "I'll be there for emotional support, if nothing else."

"You're just here to report back everything that transpires to your Kaiserina," Birbal said.

"And as a character witness," Klaven said. "Maybe I can take the heat off Gage with a few well-placed barbs to that old fart."

"Sir, please don't," said Rapoto, his Genevan guard.

"Why doesn't your man ever nursemaid you, Gage?" Klaven asked.

"Because I don't need to," Thorvald said.

"Walked right into that one, didn't I?" Klaven turned and walked backwards to take in the cityscape. "What a blight. I swear this rain is acidic and will eat right through my dress uniform."

They continued to a walled building where the corners of the tile roof were raised and drones carrying powerful floodlights and machine guns patrolled the perimeter. Farther ahead, tall walls—the top lost to the fog—loomed like a fortress.

"And that's one of the Emperor's smaller palaces," Klaven said. "It's good to be the King."

He gave Gage a wink as they entered the smaller building.

****

Gage walked beneath a pool of light and stopped in the middle, Thorvald just behind him. The floor was polished cobblestones, each stamped with the Emperor's dragon seal. The light from the drone overhead washed out everything around him but a ring of shadows a few yards away.

"This is a ruse," said a voice. "Cast him out."

"The invaders are here. How can we be sure he's not one of their assassins?" The words came from a speaker with a static hum.

"Gage is a true warrior." He recognized Birbal. "Not a criminal. End this nonsense."

"Albion's seat at the League is suspended," General Han said, "for reasons well-known to all of us. He must be treated as the enemy."

"I am enemy only to the Daegon," Gage said.

"They attacked without warning and occupied my home. Hounded us through the Kigali Nebula and I beat them at New Madras with the Indus and the Reich. Albion's light burns. We are one of the founding members of the League, and as regent, I—"

"You are nothing!" Han's silhouette rose from the ring of seats around Gage. "A nobody. Some upstart that inherited a command and got lucky. You are no regent and Albion is dead. You understand me? It died when the Daegon took your King and—"

Gage snatched Thorvald's carbine off his back and swung the muzzle straight up. Bullets ripped through the drone hovering overhead and glass rained down toward Gage.

Thorvald shot an arm over the Commodore and the armor plates fanned out to make a shield, deflecting the shards and also the drone when it crashed down. Gage passed the carbine back to the Genevan as his eyes adjusted to the ambient lighting.

Shin and Han sat next to each other. The military man looked furious, the elderly one almost amused. Next to Shin was an onyx-skinned woman with short hair and gaudy-colored robes. Beside her was Birbal, then a man with a metal face and hair of spun gold. The Mechanix barely moved, his augmented eyes clicking with each blink. Next to him was a blond-haired, blue-eyed man that sat with his arms crossed over an olive-drab uniform.

Rapoto had an arm across Klaven's chest, like a mother protecting a child after they were nearly in a car accident.

Empty rows circled the floor like an arena.

"Albion is free," Gage said to Han. "Doesn't matter if there's an enemy controlling our earth and skies. We do not bow to anyone."

"I believed that once," Han said, "and that cost me—and Cathay—dearly. I will not make the same mistake again."

"Gentlemen," Shin said, raising his hands, "I think we're all operating on incomplete information. Perhaps we were a bit overzealous in suspending Albion from the League. All in favor of restoring Gage's rights until the end of this session?"

All but Klaven and the man in the olive-drab uniform rapped their knuckles on the lacquer row in front of them.

"Gage…tell us what happened to Albion." Shin settled back into his seat. "From your perspective. Please."

Gage laid out the assassination of Admiral Sartorius and the rest of his fleet captains, the Daegon's initial assault on New Siam, their journey through the Kigali Nebula, and then the reunification with Albion ships traveling with the *Castle Itter*.

"We've heard the rest." Shin looked over at Birbal, who nodded quickly. "But Prince Aidan is…"

"Alive," Gage said. "Safe aboard my fleet."

"And with the Genevan behind you, I'm inclined to believe you really are the legitimate regent," Shin said, stroking the edge of his long goatee. "But the boy has several years to go before he can take the full crown. What's the age for an Albion royal?"

"It won't be any time soon," Gage said.

"Commodore," the dark-skinned woman said, "I am Ambassador Chibinobim Waje of the Biafura Republic. These Daegon…are they even human?"

"We've examined several of their bodies,"

Gage said. "They're just as human as we are, though their DNA has been altered to give them blue or green skin as some sort of response to a high-radiation environment. Their language seems to be Latin-based. My intelligence agents believe they're connected to a colony mission that left Earth shortly before the Edziza disaster that knocked the home world into an ice age almost a thousand years ago."

"There was no such mission," the blue-eyed man said. "It took hundreds of years before we could even leave the solar system."

"And yet the Daegon are here," Gage said. "My astrogation teams examined the slip-stream data our defenders captured during the initial invasion of Albion. Back traces point to the Veil."

"Impossible," the metal man said. "No slip travel can go through the Veil. It's a dead zone."

Gage stared at him.

"But they are human," Waje said. "This brings the Daegon into better focus."

"We've been shot with an arrow," Shin said. "We can worry about what the shooter had for breakfast or we can treat the wound."

"What else has your intelligence agent discovered?" asked the blue-eyed man, leaning forward slightly.

"I don't know you," Gage said. "By your uniform, you're from Columbia."

"He arrived just before you did," Shin said. "Impressive that he made it so far from home so quickly."

"Deacon Meers," he said. "Columbia maintains an embassy in League space. I'm here as an observer."

"Columbia couldn't be bothered to take part in the Reach Wars, but here you are now," Gage said.

"Our worlds are across the gap between this part of the galaxy and the Perseus arm," Meers said. "Settled according to prophecy. If the Hierophant wished us to take part in conflict between nonbelievers, we would have fought. Your spy?"

"I've told you everything we've learned," Gage said. "My agent is…otherwise occupied."

"Then the Daegon must be an offshoot of humanity," the metal man said, his jaw never moving, his words coming from a speaker built into the bottom of his chin. "Perhaps a colony settled by some alien race that—"

"Give up your ridiculous theories, Sokalus," Shin said. "The Daegon are here to rule us, by their own words. That 'novis regiray' they keep broadcasting. We have this League precisely for this reason."

"Our League isn't against the Daegon." Waje gave Klaven a side-eyed glance. "At least, that's how my president reads the treaty."

"It was founded for mutual defense," Gage said. "To provide a unified front against—"

"Enough!" General Han slapped a palm against the lacquer. "He's had his chance to speak. Now let him answer for Albion's crimes."

"He has a point." Shin wagged his gold-tipped fingernail next to his face. "Show Gage."

Han tapped at a desk and the lights dimmed.

A holo projected around Gage and Thorvald. Albion ships emerged from slip space and flew toward a desert world. Cathay ships formed a multi-tiered wall in orbit over a domed city as transports rose from the planet. The Albion craft settled into high anchor between the Cathay and the world.

"Basai," Han said. "Mining colony on the Albion frontier. Two million people lived in that dome. The system commander ordered a full evacuation after news of the Daegon assault first reached us. Sensible. We believed the Albion were still our allies then. They arrived and claimed they'd just outrun the Daegon at Theonis and needed sanctuary. We granted it. Like fools."

As the Albion ships at anchor began to slowly drift apart, Gage watched and touched a battleship, the same class as his *Orion*. A wall of Cathay text he couldn't read came up, with the exception of one word in English: *Heracles*. Flagship of the 5th Fleet.

A recording played over the holo.

"Admiral Nix, you're leaving your anchorage," Han said.

"Roger, we're conducting a standard reactor purge and there's a minimum safe distance required," a woman said. Gage's heart skipped a beat as he recognized the voice.

Gage nodded and said, "That is our procedure."

"Skipping ahead half an hour," Han said and the Albion ships spread out faster, stopping in a dome shape with the *Heracles* at the top.

"Albion, we're picking up a slip-space disturbance," the recording of Han continued. *"This consistent with what you saw on Theonis?"*

No response.

"Albion ships, I repeat: we're picking up—"

Torpedoes launched off the *Heracles* and swarmed a Cathay carrier. The rest of the Albion fleet opened fire, smashing unshielded vessels in seconds.

Audio of panicked Cathay language cut over the battle as a Daegon fleet came out of slip space near the planet's sole moon and joined the battle. The Cathay fleet, under fire from two directions, lurched into action too slowly to put up a real defense.

Gage watched silently as the massacre unfolded.

A few Cathay ships managed to break out of the trap and fled toward a slip-space point.

The Daegon and Albion ships did not give chase. Instead, they formed a cordon over the dome city and opened fire as one. Transport ships that

Gage knew carried civilians were destroyed without mercy. The dome cracked and exploded after a brief bombardment and the atmosphere contained within formed a giant plume that caught in the planet's wind and stretched into a white streak across the sky.

The Cathay navy ships blinked into slip space and the recording froze.

"No survivors from the colony," Han said. "No ships made it from there to Lantau or any of our stars. I hoped the Daegon and their Albion allies would give chase to me and my squadron, give the civilians a chance…but they decided to attack the helpless targets instead. Why, Gage? Why did your people do this to us?"

"It may not be the Albion," Waje said. "Perhaps the Daegon captured the vessels and put their own crews aboard."

"It was us," Gage said. "I know Admiral Nix. Everything I saw was consistent with how we fight. There's no way the Daegon could walk aboard our ships and crew them exactly like our sailors."

"An answer, Gage!" Han rose to his feet.

"I don't have one," said the Commodore as

he walked through the holo toward Han and Shin. "Admiral Nix is a veteran. A fine commander. I don't know why she would do this."

"Perhaps King Randolph is alive and surrendered to the Daegon?" Shin asked.

"He's dead," Thorvald spoke up. "I was there when it happened."

"Do you wish to see more holos?" Birbal raised a hand high. "Of Gage and his fleet gutting the Daegon assault over New Madras? Of them fighting and dying to save a world not their own?"

"No one doubts your word, Indus," Shin said. "But the issue here is …"

"The Daegon are tyrants," Gage said. "They must have threatened Nix to force her to—"

"They threatened you," Han said. "You didn't surrender."

"We do not…" Gage's face contorted with emotion, then he ran his hand down his cheeks to force his features back into neutral.

"No simple explanations," Shin said, leaning forward and looking down at Gage. "No simple solutions. Albion has attacked the Cathay,

Commodore. The Emperor knows of this. He will not be pleased to see you when he arrives with the Golden Fleet."

"Cathay has a way of dealing with traitors," Han said.

"My command has held true to Albion," Gage said. "I am no traitor. Nor the men and women with me."

"Klaven," said the Columbian, crossing his legs and leaning back, "any issue with the Albion strays you picked up?"

"Other than one eating all my Black Forest cake, no," the Reichsman said. "The Daegon arrived in system with us and those ships exited with me. No stabs in my back."

"A rogue element within the Albion command?" Waje asked. "Perhaps this Nix is one of the infiltrators that Gage spoke of."

"I don't believe so," Gage said. "All we've encountered were junior-ranked individuals in the crew. Easier to avoid detection when you have a low profile."

"Now…" Shin began, twirling the end of his

goatee around his pinky, "I can accept that Gage is not a Daegon agent."

"I do not," Han said. "The Emperor will arrive soon. We cannot risk his safety."

"And I must agree to that," Shin said.

"What? No!" Gage balled his fists. "Albion needs the League. We need your fleets to liberate our home. The treaty is—"

"Treaty?" Han asked. "The Daegon are a threat like we've never encountered before. You want us to put our own worlds at risk to free Albion? This is a trap! You're here to draw our forces into an assault on Albion and you'll lead us into the Daegon's jaws. Again!"

"I am the regent, and as head of state, I swear that is not true. The Albion who attacked you have gone rogue," Gage said. "You have to give me the chance to—"

"We owe you nothing!" Han roared. He pointed at Gage and his mouth kept moving, spit flecking off his lips as he gestured hard.

Gage's brow furrowed.

"Cone of silence." Shin twisted a ring on one

of his claw-like fingers. "His anger's justified…but he's being rude."

Han slammed a fist against the lacquered wood and seethed at Gage. His mouth moved, then his eyes narrowed. He looked at Shin and spoke wordlessly to the older man.

"A moment," Shin said as he clicked his ring to one side and the two Cathay spoke to each other without sound.

"The Daegon have taken more territory in months than changed hands since humanity left the solar system," Meers said, "and you beat them. Is that one defeat why they've stopped their advance?"

"I don't know what you mean," Gage said.

Meers tapped at controls and the holo field changed to a flat star map of the League. A swath of red spread over Albion, then grew larger and larger with passing days, the thrust of the Daegon advance pointing toward Earth. The calendar ticked several more times without the Daegon's territory increasing.

"They slowed after New Madras," Meers said. "Perhaps you took out a leadership target."

"I helped," Klaven said. "Let's not forget the

Reich's contribution."

Birbal cleared his throat loudly and Meers nodded at him.

"The one Daegon leader I've encountered is named Tiberian," Gage said. "He was obsessed with tracking down Prince Aidan. He was at Madras, but he was on the surface when the tide turned in orbit."

"*Tiberian*," said Meers. "Curious."

"And what is Columbia's concern?" Gage asked. "You've a moat of many light-years between your nation and the League. Somehow I doubt it will stop the Daegon."

"The Hierophant is divinely guided," Meers said. "I don't know what course of action has been revealed to him."

"Gage?" Shin said as Han stormed out of the chamber. "Sorry for the interruption."

"Then let us get to the point," Gage said. "I formally invoke Article VII of the League's charter. Mutual defense is—"

"Article VII can't be decided now," Shin said.

"Are we not all representatives of the treaty members?" Gage looked across the attendees.

"The Cathay Empire stipulated that any decision leading to armed conflict resides with the Emperor," Shin said. "Biafura does what they want to do and the Indus—"

"The Indus Republic has already declared war on the Daegon." Birbal stood up. "We are with Albion and will support any operation to liberate their worlds."

"President Buhari has our military on high alert," Waje said. "He is…awaiting more information."

"And your authority to act for Albion is a bit…tenuous, Gage," Shin said. "I have to reread the representation requirements to see if—"

"You wish Prince Aidan to be here?" Gage asked. "He's a boy. A boy that saw his parents slaughtered in front of him. A boy who's been hunted by assassins and monsters across the stars. What difference will it make if he demands Article VII or I do?"

"It matters to the Emperor," Shin said, "who will be most displeased when he learns how Albion ships have turned against him."

"Those ships—"

"They bear your colors," Shin said. "Gave your codes. Abused our trust to betray and murder our people. I don't mean to sound like Han, but this is how the Emperor will see things."

Gage gripped the pommel of his sword. He knew he was at a dead end…but there might be another way to salvage this.

"Then I will bring them to account," Gage said. "The 5th Fleet is still at Basai, correct?"

"According to our intelligence, yes," Shin said, his eyes twinkling.

"Then I will go to Basai and arrest Admiral Nix for treason. She is in command. This is her responsibility," Gage said.

"By Cathay law, all officers that—"

"And in Albion, we do not engage in mass punishment," Gage said.

Shin smoothed out his goatee. "I am in no position to make demands of you, Gage," he said. "But if you deal with this renegade faction…it will go far in the eyes of the Emperor."

"Give me slip codes to Basai," Gage said.

"We will leave immediately."

"The *Arjan Singh* will go with him," Birbal said. "We will host a Cathay observer as our guest."

"You mean I can get rid of Han for a while?" Shin asked. "Twist my arm. Agreed. I'll have the codes sent to the *Orion*. And as for you," he added, pointing at Klaven, "out."

"Beg your pardon?" the Reichsman asked.

"Out. Get back to your ship and leave Cathay space. I'll sign papers that will guarantee you free passage back to Reich territory. After the last war, the Emperor hates you goose-stepping shitkickers more than anything. He'll listen to reason with Gage and the Indus. You…I know what he'll do to you—and to me—for letting you pollute our skies with your presence. Out."

Klaven opened his mouth to protest, then nodded quickly.

"Gage, *juk nei hoe wan* is what we say here," Shin said. "Come back with Nix…or don't come back at all, is my advice to you."

Gage bowed slightly.

"Now shoo." Shin waved a hand at him.

"You have no idea how goddamn busy I am."

****

Thorvald stood with his feet mag-locked to the Reich shuttle as it took off from the Lantau spaceport, while Gage sat in conference with Birbal. Klaven had a hand to one ear and spoke into a receiver built into a watch. The other Genevan was on the other side of the bay, disinterested in anything but Klaven's safety.

"Grynau," Thorvald spoke into his helmet, the words silent to everyone else but his AI. "Grynau, you have to let me tell Gage."

+No+

The AI spoke with force directly to his mind.

"You were there. If he has the authority of the King, then the League will give him more authority."

+Biometric information will not be shared+

"It…this is ridiculous. If he knows he's Aidan's half-brother, what's the harm?"

+Restricted+

"Why? Why can't Gage know who he is?"

+Restricted+

"Worst-case situation is that we'll be forced to expose Aidan to the Cathay. Keep him out of danger and let Gage act with the full authority of the King...Grynau? Grynau, is this acceptable?"

The AI was silent for a full minute.

+Restricted+

Thorvald's fist struck the bulkhead, earning looks from the passengers.

"Tough decisions all around," Thorvald said to himself. "It's up to us to make the least worse one."

Chapter 8

Tiberian slipped out of silk sheets and picked up a crystal glass filled with amber liquid. He took a drink as he went to a tall window overlooking the *Sphinx* and New Exeter.

"Come back," Asaria said, beckoning Tiberian to the space next to her on the bed.

"The news from Concord…" He took another sip.

"Fanatics." She pulled a pillow beneath her head. "Lord Eubulus knew the planet's reputation and ignored it. He should have scorched the planet from orbit and been done with it. The population was more trouble than it would be worth to make them into thralls."

"Concord was never part of the High Houses' plan," Tiberian said. "The losses there were not expected. But Albion…this planet is ours now. They took such pride in being free on the edge of what they considered civilized space. Pride in their role in the little squabbles between the feral nations. This world is bent to us. The rest of the ferals know this now. The Reich, the Cathay…the fear will spread."

"Concord ended as the ferals would expect," Asaria said. "But the Reich…I will create a new writ for you. If the Kaiserina does not bend the knee to us, then you will hunt her and her family down as you did with the Albion royals."

"A challenge," Tiberian said as he half turned and raised his glass to her. "The Reich is a larger empire and the populace is just as loyal to that crown as the Albion were. When can I begin?"

"Not until the other High Houses arrive," she said. "If we attack the Reich now, we'll be in a fight of attrition. House Red Shield wants the Reich for itself…let them bleed for it, not us."

"Red Shield will give me free rein to hunt the Kaiserina?" Tiberian asked.

"They will if they want to come through my Oculus," Asaria said.

"What of the last of the Albion? Gage has proven to be a problem."

"He's competent but common-born." She sat up and stretched. "The rest of the ferals will eat him alive for us."

"Then I'm to remain here and just wait for the next Oculus transit?"

"The last transit," Asaria said. "The slip line will break after this next alignment. The last of the Daegon will finally be with us. You can find something to amuse you until then, can't you?"

Tiberian set the glass down and smiled at her.

"I've some ideas…"

Chapter 9

Gage got out of his seat as the Reich shuttle landed aboard the *Orion*.

"I guess this is goodbye," Klaven said. "As much as I'd like to accompany you on your mission to the Basai system…I'm already at the outer limits of conduct the Kaiserina will accept."

"I understand," Gage said, shaking his hand. "Safe journey back to the Reich."

"I'm not worried about anyone tangling with the *Castle Itter*," Klaven said. "Wish me luck when I'm back at the royal court. I'd be safer fighting the Daegon."

"It's rough all around," Gage said and walked down the ramp, stepping off and back onto the flight deck before the edge of the ramp touched down.

Price and three of his bridge officers, as well as Emma, his new porter, were waiting for him. He unbuckled his sword belt and handed the weapon to Emma as they walked to a turbo lift. Dirty crewmen stepped away from their work on fighters and shuttles to stand at attention and salute as he passed.

"We received slip-space instructions from the Kongs," said Ensign Clarke, the astrogator. "Several plots to get us to the Basai system. Do you know why—"

"Load them into the navi-computers and find us an out-system slip point," Gage said. "We need to get in without being noticed."

"But that's Daegon territory and…yes, sire. Right away." Clarke ran ahead to the bank of lifts.

"The ship's captains are assembled for Arlyss' court martial," Price said. "His counsel's already filed several motions to—"

"Later," Gage said. "Keep Arlyss in the brig. Good that the commanders are here. I need to speak to them immediately."

"Fair enough." Price swiped through several

pages on her tablet. "What's our next move? I've been working on integrating new crew that we picked up on Madras and a few are upset because they think they're overqualified for—"

Gage glanced at Wyman and Ivor as he passed by their squadron.

"We've a point of honor to address, XO," Gage said as he stepped onto a lift. "One we can't ignore."

****

"And that's all I've got," Commander Stannis of the Cobra Squadron said to his ready room full of pilots. "The Commodore has us on ready condition one, soon as we arrive in the Basai system."

"But are we fighting Daegon or…" Wyman asked, raising a hand slightly.

"We need to be prepped to engage Typhoons and Albion vessels," Stannis said and the rest of the pilots shifted around uncomfortably. "I don't like it either. But if the 5th Fleet is compromised, we have to handle them as a hostile force."

"They're our people," Ivor said. "Why would they fight us? Why won't they kumbaya like the ships we found with the Reich?"

"The 5th was just fine when the Kongs took them in…you saw what happened," Stannis said. "We have to assume they're compromised somehow."

"This ain't Reich or Indus," Wyman said. "These are our people."

"If anyone's going to hesitate on the trigger, tell me now," Stannis said. "If you're going to do your duty to King and country against those who threaten us or those that have given up their oaths of service, then be in the simulators in ten minutes. We're going up against the Falcons, and if our kill ratio isn't triple theirs, we're not leaving the sims. Now move it."

Chapter 10

Turbulence rattled the lander and Seaver pressed his helmet back against the bulkhead. The mag locks seemed to know when he needed the support and when he needed to look around. The Daegon had ample high technology, more advanced than what he'd had at home on Albion, but they reserved the best of it for themselves.

The lenses of his helmet had a degree of night vision, putting a green outline around the themata soldiers and a golden one around Juliae. A small arrow pointed toward her every time he looked away. There were no words on his HUD, just the simple indicators and a counter for the number of rounds in his machine gun and another for the magazines on his back—so simple even an uneducated peasant from the most backward world could figure it out. Seaver suspected that was the point.

A snap sounded beyond the shuttle, too sharp for thunder.

"Keoni, the ferals air defense artillery is still operational," she said over a linked network.

"The sector commander said it be dead by now, yeah?" the legio asked.

"You wish to lodge a complaint with the commander? I can arrange a face-to-face meeting if Nicias doesn't rip it off after this foul-up," Juliae said.

Seaver traded a glance with Powell. He wasn't sure if the Daegon was serious or jesting with her top soldier.

"The themata, they get scared," Keoni said.

"We're on final descent…they come down too soon, I'll hit them again. They're all young. Their hearts can take it." Juliae swiped a hand across her forearm and pads on the tips of her gloves lit up.

"No me, master. No me," the legio said.

"You don't need the rage," she said. "You're always angry." She double-tapped a screen invisible to

Seaver and there was a sharp pain at the base of his neck.

"Whoa…" Inez's head bobbled slightly.

Seaver's muscles twitched and his breathing sped up. He leaned forward against the restraints, but the bulkhead held him back. Energy flooded his body and his finger touched the machine gun's trigger.

"My teeth are humming," Powell said.

"Let's go." Inez jerked forward, like a dog on a leash wanting to give chase. "Let's just go already."

From the rows of themata, cries and shouts rose over the din of the engines. Fists pumped up and down and rifle butts whacked against the deck.

Keoni raised his rifle up and beat out a rhythm.

Bang…bang-bang.

Seaver's vision began to double.

Bang…bang-bang.

"You all serve the Daegon," Juliae said, speakers in the bottom of her helmet amplifying her voice. "You lived without the yoke for too long. Now blood will pay the price. Kill the enemy. Pay it with their blood. Save your own. Novis regiray!"

"Novis regiray!" the themata shouted back, and Seaver was shocked when he realized he'd joined in.

The deck beneath the forward rows exploded upwards, killing a dozen themata instantly. Wind roared into the troop compartment and sunlight glared through a massive rent in the deck. The shuttle tipped to one side, then lurched into a spiral.

Seaver heard Juliae shouting, but if she was giving orders, it didn't matter. The tear in the deck ripped open as the shuttle corkscrewed down. Seats came loose and hurtled through the hole, taking screaming soldiers with them.

The shuttle pulled up and a long object flew right at his face. Reaching up, he caught it with reflexes that shocked him. He thought he had a rifle in his grip, but when he pushed it away to look at it in the flickering red lights…it was a leg severed just below the hip. He tossed the limb away, his mind registering what had just happened, but his emotions deadened by the drug Juliae had given him.

"Brace for landing!" Juliae cried out.

Seaver gripped his rifle tight to his chest and

watched through the hole in the deck as a ruined cityscape sped by beneath them. Engines strained and their forward velocity cut back sharply, so fast that Seaver's left leg came loose from the magnetic moorings. He kicked it back and it locked into place.

A yellow light flared from the port side as a missile struck the shuttle's wing. The craft tipped to one side and a pair of soldiers came out of their seats, smacking into the roof with a bone-crushing thud.

The shuttle inverted and crashed a split second later.

Seaver's world went upside down as he hung there, suspended against the wall, until the mag clamps released and he landed on one shoulder. He rolled to his feet and racked a bullet into his machine gun.

"Get out, get out!" Keoni was already unbuckled and on his feet. He reached up with a knife and cut a themata from her belts, putting a hand to her shoulder as she fell and stopping her from landing on her head.

"Grab any rifle! It no matter!" Keoni pulled a stunned soldier up and shoved a weapon into his chest.

Juliae had one hand to an upside-down door. "Crew is dead," she said. "We're nowhere near our landing zone. Damn this planet."

"Orders?" Inez asked.

"Get the rest of the themata ready to fight." She put one hand to the side of her helmet. "I'll petition for support."

"You have to ask?" Powell kicked away a bloody arm.

Juliae drew her pistol and a small golden light on the side of the barrel lit up. Powell stifled a scream and went rigid.

"I do not need your input," Juliae said, her jaw clenched. "Obey. Now." The light switched off and Powell's shoulders slumped forward.

Seaver reached up and yanked on the buckle of a soldier's restraints then lowered the man easily. Seaver wasn't sure if it was the armor or his muscles that made the motion so easy, but the blubbering thanks he got from the soldier was enough to propel him on to the next trapped themata—a young woman. Her face was blue, and her long hair hung loose, dangling with her arms. Her neck was broken, a look of dull surprise frozen on her face. Seaver remembered her from the food lines. She always had a smile, no matter how bad things got. Jennifer? Jessica?

"Door!" Keoni shouted, moving away from the ramp—which had opened a few inches then ground to a halt—to an emergency hatch just large enough for an adult to get through. He tugged at a red lever and the hatch fell with a clang.

"You! Out!" Keoni grabbed a soldier by the shirt and hauled them through the opening.

Shots rang out and a bullet-riddled body fell back into the shuttle, while more weapons opened up outside and punctures stitched across the hull. Themata screamed and fell as bullets ripped through them.

The arrow on Seaver's HUD pointing to Juliae pulsed red. He lowered a shoulder and charged forward, hitting a window and breaking through the shuttle's hull into a street. His HUD flashed white outlines onto huddled shapes around a building just across the way. Planting his feet, he opened fire with his machine gun. The rounds punched through the brick walls, kicking up puffs of dust as they passed through and hit the Concord defenders on the other side.

A bullet glanced off his thigh. The impact stung, but any pain was lost to the haze of drugs in his system. Seaver fired on full auto and swept the muzzle across the second storey, shattering glass and ripping through the wall. The magazine ran empty as the white outlines retreated into the building. He ran forward, vaulting over a windowsill and into the first floor of what had been an office building. Dead Concord soldiers lay strewn about. A wounded woman crawled toward a back door, a trail of blood behind her.

Seaver dropped his empty mag and slapped in a new one from off his back. A servo in the machine gun racked the first round.

Hearing pounding footsteps on the ceiling, he fired quick bursts almost at random. The bullets knocked tiles loose and they came tumbling down amid screams of pain from above. He hurried to the wall on the other side of the room, stomping past the wounded soldier, ignoring her as she looked up at him, frozen with fear.

He heard the stomp of boots on a stairwell and crouched down.

The wounded defender was two yards away, her face pale from blood loss, one arm clenched to a ruined stomach. Seaver looked at her for a moment, his mind registering that he was the one that shot her—and the rest of the dead men and women on this level.

Part of him knew he should feel some manner of compassion for her, that he hadn't inflicted so much pain and suffering for any true reason. He'd arrived on Concord minutes ago and now he was killing strangers.

All those thoughts went away as another wave of drugs hit his system and the urge to finish her off with a stomp to the neck almost got him away from his cover.

"Run! Run back to the school!" came through the shattered window next to Seaver.

The sound of footsteps on a fire escape ceased and Seaver counted to three, popped up and brought his machine gun to his shoulder. More than a dozen Concord soldiers were running across the remains of a playground, the grass littered with hunks of masonry and glass blown out by the fighting.

Seaver felt nothing but the gun's recoil as he mowed the Concord soldiers down, watching them pitch forward or crumble to the ground as his bullets struck. One dived beneath a jungle gym, and Seaver hit him with a quick burst, splattering blood against the happy plastic animals.

The battlefield went quiet as Seaver looked for more targets, smoke rising from his barrel.

"Bastard," said the wounded woman as her head sank to the ground and a puddle of blood grew beneath her. "We won't…won't give you the satisfaction." She lifted her chin and bared her teeth at him. "Won't let you take—"

Keoni jogged past Seaver and shot her in the head.

"First and Third squad, here!" Keoni pointed his shock maul at the middle of the room and themata rushed in from the other side. "You. Back with Juliae. Never leave her side, understand?" He thrust a finger at a stairwell.

"Moving." Seaver obeyed instantly, taking the steps three at a time despite the bulk and weight of his armor.

He found Juliae crouched against a hallway, pictures of Concord real estate hanging crooked on office doors. Inez and Powell stood on either side of her, shielding her as she had one hand to her helm and her head tucked down, deep in conversation with someone.

"Clear." She slapped Inez on the thigh and he kicked open a door, sweeping his weapon across the interior. Inez crossed the hall and beat open a door with the butt of his machine gun. He cried out in joy and moved inside.

"No! No, please don't—"

Inez stomped the plea into silence and then charged into the next office.

"Good move," Powell said to Seaver. "You bought us time to get clear of the shuttle."

"Right." Seaver's hands trembled and a cold sweat broke out across his forehead. "Just…felt like the right thing to do."

"You stay with me unless I order you otherwise," Juliae said. "No initiative. Obedience."

"Yes, master," Seaver said.

"My orders are to take that indoctrination center and hold it until Lord Nicias' forces can reach us. We crashed along the main axis of advance…small favors." She stood up and motioned her pistol muzzle to the far wall. "Covering fire. Go."

"Indoctrination center…you mean the school?" Seaver asked. "The enemy's there…I think."

"Then it's worth taking." Juliae kicked him in the upper thigh just hard enough to hurt and he ran down the hallway.

Inez—his boots bloody—saw the two guards pass by as he left an office and fell in behind them.

"I like this," he said. "Feeling so good right now. Total energy. Let's find more, yeah?"

"Stay with Juliae," Powell said. "We just…just have to do what she tells us. That's all."

"Forward!" Keoni's order carried through the floor and themata swarmed out of the bottom level. They charged over the defenders Seaver had killed, and he turned his attention to the two-story school building across the playground.

Muzzle flashes popped as defenders took shots. Seaver poured fire at each place his HUD identified Concord soldiers. The combined fire from Inez and Powell put a quick stop to the threat to the themata as they crossed to the school.

Seaver heard a high-pitched whine and slammed his back to the wall just as a mortar shell struck the themata. Glancing around the window he'd been firing through, he saw a small crater surrounded by dead and dying themata.

"Rooftop," Juliae said. "With me!"

She dived through the window and rolled to her feet in a motion so smooth, Seaver was caught flat-footed. The Daegon kept running, heading to one side of the school.

"Damn it!" Seaver jumped out, stumbled hard, then followed the flashing arrow on his HUD as fast as he could, ignoring the pitiful cry of a themata clutching a severed arm and the moans of a fellow slave soldier lying on his back and reaching for the sky, his stomach and thighs a bloody ruin.

Juliae jumped up and dug her fingertips into

the school's wall. She scaled the building, the talons in her gloves and boots gouging out purchase all the way up. Seaver made for an emergency ladder, slung his weapon over one shoulder, and made his way as fast as he could.

Just as Juliae disappeared over the edge, there was another *bloop* of the mortar firing. Seaver missed a rung and fell down a foot, catching himself before he crashed into Inez, who let off a string of expletives detailing just how slow and genetically inferior Seaver was.

At the sound of a scream, Seaver looked up and saw a Concord soldier thrown over the roof. He fell, arms flailing, and landed on his head with a meaty crunch. Seaver hurried up the ladder and rolled over the edge to find a mortar tube lying against open ammo cases and backpacks.

Juliae stood over a soldier, lashing at his arms and chest as he screamed in pain. She hacked off part of his forearm then raised her blade up high and flung it into his chest, pinning him to the ground. She slapped hands against his ears and tore his head clean off in one smooth motion.

Seaver stood motionless, stunned at the brutality as she tossed the head up, caught it by the hair, and flung it away.

"That…" she said, pointing to the mortar tube with one hand while she flapped blood off the other.

Seaver put a foot against the base plate and wrenched the tube out, then slammed it against his knee, bending it in half as he looked out across the city. Beneath the sky choked with smoke from countless small fires was a massive structure with columns and a large central dome, reminiscent of old North American capitals. There were miles between the Hexen and Juliae and her themata…and Concord was going to fight for every inch of it.

"They're retreating." Inez tapped the side of his helmet and hurried over to Juliae. "I'm picking up their movement a few blocks away. Let me go and—"

A red crater blew out of his back and his machine gun clattered to the roof.

The sound of the sniper's shot caught up to the bullet strike as Inez slumped to his knees, head bobbing from side to side, then pitched forward.

Dead.

Seaver put himself between Juliae and his best guess as to the sniper's location and pulled her back to the ladder.

She grabbed him by the shoulder and yanked him down just as a bullet snapped overhead. Keeping her grip, she jumped off the roof, dragging him along.

The dead soldier she'd thrown off earlier didn't look big enough to cushion his fall. The still rational part of his brain tried to panic, but his emotions remained comfortably numb as he fell. Juliae caught the ladder and she swung Seaver into it. He fumbled with a rung, held on for dear life, then looked up, locking his gaze with Juliae. She hung against the ladder with the ease of a circus acrobat.

"Keoni's secured the indoctrination center," Juliae said. "Get inside. Recover the other's weapon and ammo later. That sniper isn't overly talented, but there's no need to take the risk right now."

"No talent?" Seaver made his way down the ladder and jumped off while still a few feet above the ground. "He killed Inez."

"You think he was aiming for that one?"

Juliae landed with barely a sound. "I'm insulted."

"No, Master, I meant—"

"Both of you had best keep up next time I decide to stretch my legs." Juliae snapped her fingers and walked through the broken double doors of the school and into the cafeteria like she owned the place.

Inside, her themata broke down tables and old equipment to reinforce the walls, turning the school into a bunker.

Keoni went down a line of wounded. He knelt next to a woman gasping through a sucking chest wound and put his hand to her forehead. A metal bolt shot out from beneath his wrist and crushed her skull. He jerked his hand free and went to the next, a teenager with a belt tied around the stump of one arm. Keoni finished him off with the bolt and kept going.

"We can't…we can't do something for them?" Powell asked.

"The legio's mercy is 'something,'" Juliae said. "No medics. No support. They are less of a burden to the mission now that they're dead. Their weapons and ammo go to those that can still fight. There a problem?"

"No, master." Powell shook her head.

"Don't want the legio's mercy? Don't get wounded," Juliae said. "The rest of the themata know this now. They'll fight harder. You," she pointed at Seaver, "make sure the entire perimeter is covered by eyes and guns. Anyone fires on the Daegon sent to recover me out of panic or ill-discipline will be executed. Accident or not."

"Yes, master." Seaver beat a fist to his upper chest as he'd seen her do with other officers and went for a stairwell.

****

Bullets ripped through a window, sending bits of wood and glass zipping through the room. A themata rolled away from his spot against the wall as rounds punched through, chasing him as he scrambled toward a file cabinet providing cover for three other soldiers. He yelped in pain and clutched an arm to his chest, rolling away from the wall.

Seaver charged into the room and slid to a

stop at the window, aiming his machine gun as bullets pinged off his armor. Seaver let off quick bursts, demolishing a low wall across the street, then lunged to one side, dodging a sniper's bullet that whacked against the floor and kicked out a small crater.

He jumped over the themata cowering behind the cabinet and ducked next to the window. He paused, then swung his rifle through the window and cut down a team of five Concord soldiers as they fled away from the wall he'd just broken down.

Flashing his middle finger out the window, Seaver jumped to one side and backed toward the wounded themata, ear cocked for the sound of the sniper's next shot.

"Maybe he's low on ammo," Seaver thought out loud as his heels backed against the themata, who cried out in fear.

"I can still fight! I can, swear it!" the young man shouted.

Seaver looked down. The themata had a bullet wound clear through his forearm. Blood seeped through his fingers, pulsing with each heartbeat. Seaver swung his rifle onto his back and knelt down next to the casualty as he pulled a medical pouch out of the man's gear. The themata looked at him with wide eyes, jaw quivering.

"I'm not the legio," he said, tearing the pack open and removing a dense roll of fiber. "It's me, Seaver. Albion."

"What the hell did they do to you?" the man asked as Seaver twisted the fiber open along a seam and stretched it out into a band the width of his hand. He pulled the man's sleeve up and slapped the kit onto the entry wound. Blood seeped into the fabric and ran down his arm as Seaver wrapped it around, covering the bloody hole on the underside. He squeezed and the fabric tightened on its own.

He wasn't sure how the Daegon kits worked, but they managed to stop both the bleeding from anything but a severed artery and the pain from most wounds. He'd seen them stretched out to cover burns over most of a themata's back and used to cap dismembered limbs.

"They call it 'shaped,'" Seaver said. "You still have feeling in that hand?"

"I can fight. Just don't tell the legio about

me," the man said.

"You're not going to hide that." Seaver stood up and unslung his rifle.

"He's not," Keoni said from the doorway. He had a lit cigarette in the corner of his mouth and a small box in one hand.

"Centurion Juliae say Daegon almost here. Sharp eyes. You shoot at them, you get a bullet." He slapped the back of his head, then clicked a button on the box and a pill dropped into his hand. "All themata, take Uptick." He tossed a pill at each wounded soldier, who dry swallowed it without hesitation. After passing out the pills, Keoni whacked Seaver on the arm as he left, signaling for him to follow.

"Why you up here?" Keoni asked as they made their way down a hallway, dead Concord soldiers pressed against the walls to keep a passageway open. Stopping next to one near the stairwell, he rifled through the corpse's pockets.

"They were under fire. Juliae allowed me to—"

"You ask to help themata." Keoni slapped a

thigh pocket on the body and his eyes lit up. "Just themata. They die. That's what they're for." He pulled a bloodstained pack of cigarettes from the pocket and wiped it against the dead man's pants.

"They're...Albion, like me, Legio," Seaver said. "The more of us alive to fight, the better we'll fight as a themata. Yeah?"

Keoni shook the pack and individual cigarettes popped out of the open side. He pulled them out one by one, tossing away any stained with blood and tucking clean ones into another pack he produced from his belt.

"You're low," Keoni said. "Think too much. You worry about Juliae, maybe me if you have time." He took a final drag on the cigarette in his mouth and flicked the butt away. "You smoke? No. You find more, you give them to me, yeah? Now go back to Juliae."

The bark of rifle fire cut down the hallway. Seaver turned back, but Keoni slapped him on the back of the head.

"Not your job," Keoni said. "All those feral dead out there, big keep-away sign for others. No worry about themata. Worry about Juliae."

"Yes, Legio." Seaver went down the stairs to the cafeteria, where the Daegon sat on an old table. Powell stood to one side, while a pile of ammunition and themata rifles were to one side of Juliae.

She motioned at Seaver with two clawed fingertips. "Kneel," she said as one hand swiped over her forearm and she tapped at a holo Seaver couldn't see. He went to one knee, careful to keep his muzzle off the ground and away from pointing at her, even for a moment.

The back of Seaver's helmet pinched and a chill spread from the port on his collarbone.

"Your shaping hasn't cured fully, but your body's taking to the change well enough," she said. "We normally give you all a few more days so that your system balances just right...your skin shade may shift over the next few days. Pay it no mind."

A jolt of cold shot through his chest, and his mind swam as endorphins flooded his bloodstream.

"Now let's get you poised." Her finger did a double tap and the euphoria melted away, replaced by a crystal-clear focus. His vision sharpened and he thought he heard Keoni berating someone upstairs.

"Is this…Uptick?" he asked.

"No, you're on a whole different mélange of stims," she said. "Don't take the themata's pills—it'll offset your system. You don't want to come down in the middle of a fight."

Juliae stood up and removed the magazine from her pistol. She flicked rounds out and they landed in a neat line on the table. Seaver wasn't sure how she managed the feat and worried that whatever drugs she had him on were causing hallucinations.

"I hate waiting." She picked up the bullets— each a small power pack—and examined them before her lenses before reloading. "Our way of war is not the protracted siege. We establish dominance. Control the orbitals. Demand surrender. If a feral planet refuses, we bomb cities until they surrender or there are no more cities left. Then we garrison what's left and move on to the next planet. Lightning war. This…this is not how things are done."

"Then…why, Centurion?" Seaver asked.

"Concord has a reputation. Lord Nicias…either he didn't know because the specters sent to gather intelligence on this world failed at their task and should be flayed alive. Or he knows that they took this 'live free or die' credo far too seriously and this assault is done solely to break their will and send a message to other feral leadership castes."

She reloaded the rest of the bullets with an almost angry speed.

"But this is one of those 'wild space' worlds, isn't it?" she asked Seaver.

"Concord is nonaligned," he said. "It was never considered as lawless as the rest of the fringe. Pirate clans weren't allowed passage through the system...but a lot of pirates showed up at the ports to buy and sell."

"They had no treaties with other worlds? Not like your Albion and the Indus. They weren't in the League?" Juliae asked.

"No, master," Powell said.

"Then this system could have been bypassed," Juliae said. "The pirate clans haven't attacked us; they're not stupid. Concord wasn't that stupid either. Lord Nicias is here to build his reputation, kiss up to Lord Eubulus...and we're the ones paying the blood price."

Juliae slapped the magazine back into her pistol.

"Albion fell quickly to us," she said. "Surprise was total. That is how the Daegon meant to execute this re-conquest…yet here we are. But there is opportunity here. I follow my orders, command my themata…victory is inevitable. Those less capable than I will fall by the wayside. Soon I will be in a position to make better decisions."

"And…them?" Seaver cocked his head to his fellow slave soldiers.

"Keep me alive and you'll rise with me," she said. "Keoni's done very well for himself. Won't be long before—"

"Golems!" a themata called out from a wall.

Seaver looked down at his rifle, then back out a window, unsure if what he saw was friend or foe.

"Right on time," Juliae said.

A massive fist punched through a wall, knocking cinder blocks and dust loose. Targeting lasers cut through the gray dust and shouts of fear rose through the themata.

Seaver recalled fighting the things on Albion—though "fighting" may have been the wrong word. Memories of glimpsing the golems as they tore through buildings, ripped defenders apart, and annihilated trees with firepower of a walking tank were full of fear…but there was no fear now. The Daegon must have taken that emotion from him.

Juliae grabbed her forearm and rotated the armor plate back and forth. The targeting lasers cut out and the dust cleared around the golem.

The thing was eight feet tall, its helmet a simple dome with a line across the middle. Its chassis was humanoid, with wide shoulders and narrow legs, and it carried a massive machine gun with bullets the size of a man's hand in an ammo belt connected to its back. Old blood caked the golem's feet and hands. It almost looked like a man could fit inside, if he was already enormous. The golem was sealed off, no hint of any flesh beneath the armor. Though it stood slightly different than he'd seen worker robots, this golem had a stature and its own gait as it entered the cafeteria.

A holo lens flickered on its torso and Lord

Nicias' head and shoulders appeared before Juliae.

"Enjoy the rest?" Nicias asked. Seaver heard the true Daegon language beneath the translation that was louder in his ears.

"We've been in constant contact since we took this facility," Juliae said. "My casualties—"

"Themata are a resource to be expended, Centurion," Nicias said. "The advance on the Hexen continues. You'll join the 14th Regiment in its assault on a residential area just east of your current location. I need the highway clear for walkers. I've lost too many to potshots from bypassed ferals. Don't get too used to the golems. They have another target."

"By your will, my lord," Juliae said.

Seaver looked at her, expecting some degree of pushback. Advancing behind the golems—three more stomped past the school as the two Daegon spoke—was a more tactically sound plan.

"Operation plan follows." Nicias' holo flickered through a rainbow of colors, and data scrolled up Juliae's lenses.

Nicias vanished, and the golem marched forward. It lumbered past the table with the weapons and ammo, pushing it aside with one swipe of its leg, then punched through the other side of the cafeteria and back out onto the street.

"Legio," Juliae said, tracing a circle in the air next to her face, "we advance. Any not on their feet and ready to move in three minutes will be left behind. What the Concordians do to any they find will be far worse than the peace you might give them."

She tossed magazines recovered from Inez's body to her two shaped. "Take all you can carry," she said. "You'll need it."

Chapter 11

Gage walked into his quarters, Emma one step behind, and unsnapped the clasp on his high collar. Thorvald took up his normal position outside in the passageway. The regent breathed a sigh of relief as cool air flooded through his tunic, and he took a seat at a small table where a steaming plate of scrambled eggs and bacon waited for him.

Emma lifted up his foot and yanked a boot off.

"I can do that myself, thank you," he said.

"Sooner I have you comfortable, the sooner you can get some food and rest, sire," she said. "Got to refresh your dress uniform and redo the polish to keep you presentable."

"Emma?" Gage frowned at the plate of food. "How is this still warm when you were there when I landed?"

"That'd be me, sire." Bertram stuck his head out of the doorway leading to a small kitchen and closets.

"Mr. Bertram," Emma said, putting her hands on her hips, "I'm the Commodore's steward. There's no need for you to—"

"Gage?" Prince Aidan came out from behind Bertram and rubbed sleep from his eyes.

"Our young master didn't care for his quarters," Bertram said, a hint of sadness in his voice. "He wanted to be in the closet where we've taken shelter during battle stations. Salis is back here with us."

"Please join me." Gage motioned to the other open seat at the table and Aidan climbed up and sat across. "More bad dreams?"

Aidan nodded.

"Well, we won't be in this system for much longer." Gage picked up a fork then looked at the bare spot in front of Aidan.

"Bertram, we need—"

The other porter came out with a bowl of brightly colored cereal and set it in front of the boy. Aidan took a greedy bite and smiled at Gage.

"Not the most nutritious choice, but at least you're eating," Gage said.

"Are you going to send me to the Kong planet?" Aidan asked.

"Who taught you that word?" Gage ate some of his eggs.

"Mr. Berty. He said the Kongs will sell their own mothers for a shilling if they feel like it," Aidan said.

Bertram ducked his head and slipped back into the kitchen.

"They are the Cathay. That's what you should call them, my Prince," Gage said.

"Are you sending me there?"

"No…no, we don't have an embassy on Lantau. And even if we did, I'd rather have you aboard the *Orion*. It's safe—it's better for everyone."

"That's good. So where are we going? I feel the engines rumbling."

Gage set his fork down. "There's a problem in Basai. Some Albion ships are…they're not fighting for the right side, my Prince. And I have to go and find out why."

"They're with the bad guys?" the boy asked.

Gage nodded slowly.

"Why do we have to do it? If they're with the bad guys…won't there be more bad guys there?"

"That is a concern, but we'll be careful," Gage said. "As for why it has to be us…we are Albion, Aidan. You are the kingdom's light, and what these other ships are doing hurts who we are. Albion does not fight beside oppressors. We can't let them do this."

"Maybe they're tricked," Aidan said. "A wizard put a spell on their brains, maybe."

"Maybe," Gage said.

"What if I say no?" Aidan asked. "Salis promised I'll be King one day, then I can stop taking yucky vitamins and eat chicken all the time. Can I be King now?"

"It would be a load off my back," Gage sighed. "Say you were King. Would we go and stop the other Albion ships that are helping the Daegon?"

Aidan shifted in his seat. "Are people going to get hurt?"

"They might. But the Daegon aren't afraid to hurt anyone."

"If we stop the others…maybe they'll help us like the ships the Krauts brought to us?"

There was a clatter of dropped pots from the kitchen, and Gage made a mental note to speak with Bertram about his choice of words around the boy.

"That's the best way for things to work out," Gage said.

"And if they don't want to be on our side?"

"Then…I can't let them stay with the Daegon," the Commodore said.

Aidan poked his spoon into his cereal. "But if you get them on our side…we can go home sooner?" he asked, his eyes lighting up.

"Yes, my Prince, I hope that's what will happen."

"Then we should go get them." Aidan rapped his spoon on the table and sent flecks of milk across Gage's plate.

"As you command," Gage said and took a bite of his eggs.

"Do I have to go talk to the Cattys?" Aidan asked. "Their Emperor is a kid like me."

"He's a bit older than you," Gage said, "but you let me deal with the Cathay, OK?"

"But Mr. Bertram says the Cattys only like royal people. Anyone else and they like to—"
He ran a finger across his neck.

"The young master overheard me speaking to Salis." Bertram peeked around the doorway. "I'll be much more careful in the future, sir."

"The Cathay aren't like that," Gage said. "Let's have a race to see who can finish our food first, OK? Ready. Set."

Gage took a big bite of eggs and chewed as Aidan squealed in protest and lifted up a spoonful of cereal.

****

Outside Gage's quarters and using his armor's sensors, Thorvald listened to the Commodore and

130

Aidan's conversation. He opened a suit-to-suit channel to Salis.

"Gage needs to know," Thorvald said.

"No he doesn't. We've been over this."

"You weren't down there, Salis. You didn't see how they treated Gage."

"I'm sure the Albion ships fighting alongside the Daegon had more to do with it than anything."

"If he's not the King, they'll dismiss him."

"Not. Our. Problem. We're here to keep them safe, not meddle in their affairs. I shouldn't have to explain this to you, Thorvald. We're trained to avoid attachment to the principals. I know your contract is nearly up and you spent so long with the Albion, but be a professional. That's who we are as Genevans—as representatives of House Ticino."

+She's right+ his AI said to him.

"You're both missing the bigger picture," Thorvald said.

"We don't have a 'bigger picture.' We only have our mission."

Thorvald cut the channel, his mind struggling with the decision before him.

****

Ensign Gage followed Captain Royce through the halls of the New Exeter palace. He glanced at his meager ribbon bar in a mirror as they passed and adjusted the silver and gold cord on his shoulder for the umpteenth time.

The Genevan was massive, and Gage wasn't sure if the perception was due to the armor or the imposing presence the chief of royal security emanated. He heard the faintest whir from the armor's servos as it moved.

"You're aware of the appropriate greetings?" Royce asked.

"Yes, Captain. I meant to rehearse with my section chief aboard the Starfire, but I didn't have—"

"You're not here, Ensign," Royce said. "You never were here. You will never tell anyone about this. Understood?"

"I understand your instructions," Gage said. "Just not the…reasons for them."

"Politics," Royce stated. "Your naval officers are a unique bunch."

"I may not have gone to Sanquay, but I know how to follow orders," Gage said.

Royce stopped at a floor-to-ceiling painting of a mountain range on the eastern continent and the T-line on his helmet flashed. He touched the picture frame and it swung off the wall with a click. The Genevan motioned Gage into a dark space and closed a vault door behind him.

Gage stood in absolute darkness for a moment, his heart pounding, then a line of light appeared in front of him. He reached out and pushed a heavy door open.

King Randolph was in the next room, seated at an oak desk carved with the planet Albion's hemisphere on one side, a wreath around the planet. The King wore a button-down shirt, and a small crown sat on a velvet dome to one side of the desk.

The man stared hard at a data slate, a frown on his lips.

Gage raised a foot and stomped it against the floor, then brought one hand up to salute.

"Cad—Ensign Thomas Gage of Your Majesty's Ship Starfire reporting as ordered," Gage said.

The King sat up and set the slate down. He looked at Gage for a moment, then a slow smile crossed his face.

"Not a cadet anymore, are you?" Randolph stood and stretched out his arms. "Graduated from Portsmouth just last week. You're so new, you almost squeak."

"My apologies, sire," Gage said, still holding his salute.

Randolph returned the salute quickly and motioned Gage over. Gage marched forward and stood at rigid attention in front of the desk. The walls were covered in shelves holding real paper books, and a portrait of Randolph's father after a successful chrome tiger hunt was directly behind the King. Gage couldn't help but appreciate the resemblance between the two men.

"Relax, relax." Randolph came around and looked over Gage's face. "You take after your mother. Your father and I served together during the Reach War. Did you know that?"

"Yes, sire. My mother showed me photos. Had stories."

"I was...so sorry that she passed," Randolph said, "but your success is a testament to how well she raised you. Graduating at the top of your class at Portsmouth is no easy feat."

"I couldn't get into Sanquay," Gage said.

"The nobles are like that." Randolph put his hands to his hips and shook his head. "They treat every institution like their own little fiefdoms. The navy needs leaders, not entitled brats that think they can drive a ship because their mommy or daddy inherited a title…or bought one."

Gage pressed his lips together, unsure what to say.

"But look at you," Randolph said. "Losing your father in battle was a dark day. I'm not supposed to look into the individual welfare of my people; gives a bad impression that I play favorites when my duty is to the people as a whole…but I kept an eye on you and your mother."

"You…did?" Gage asked.

"She was ill for some time before her passing, unable to work," Randolph said, retaking his seat. "I looked after your family's expenses. The stipend you received from age thirteen until the day you were commissioned?"

"I thought it was my father's…"

"Casualty stipends only last ten years and are half as much as you received." Randolph shrugged. "Some days it's good to be the King."

"Thank you, sire. It made a difference for us. Why…if I may be so bold, why tell me now? Why have me—"

"Snuck into the palace by my Genevans? A King has to maintain a perception, Ensign. Your mother was—your parents were very close to me. Making sure you and she were taken care of was a matter of honor for me, especially after your father was lost fighting the Reich. I was there when it happened…" Randolph got very quiet for a moment, then continued. "But if the tabloids knew what I was doing…it would lead to a scandal that would stop me from being able to help you."

"I never knew," Gage said. His brow furrowed and he frowned.

"I know where your mind's going," the King said. "Now you're rethinking every accomplishment you've achieved since you finished high school. Do you know what I had to do to ensure you graduated from the academy?"

"No, sire."

"Nothing." Randolph smiled. "You did the work. There was no hidden hand making your midshipman career easier or inflating your grades. You got yourself through, my boy. Though I wish you'd applied to Sanquay."

"That's for the nobles, sire."

"Albion has two systems," the King said, "parallel and unequal. Your naval career is just beginning, but I will promise you this, Thomas: Carry out your duties to the best of your abilities. The higher ranks aren't just for the nobility. If you're flag-rank material, you'll earn your stars."

"Because of my father?" Gage asked.

"Yes," said Randolph, the side of his mouth twitching. "Never limit yourself because you think the circumstances of your birth are against you, Thomas. I've had my eye on you for some time. And I'll keep that eye on you."

"For Albion," Gage said, "I will carry the torch. Her light burns."

"You make an old man proud." Randolph stood and shook Gage's hand. The King held the grip for a bit too long, staring at Gage, then he led the young officer back to the secret door.

Gage never saw him again.

****

Gage sat at the desk in his wardroom aboard the *Orion*. Thorvald, out of his armor and wearing simple crew fatigues, stood across from him. The low thrum of air circulators was the only sound as Gage stared at the desk.

"And you're certain?" Gage asked.

"Blood doesn't lie," Thorvald said. "My AI searched for a donor match when Aidan suffered a minor injury…you are his half-brother."

"My father died before I was born," Gage said. "My mother…never even hinted that King Randolph was…I believed her connection to the King came from his service with my father."

Thorvald let Gage contemplate in silence.

"Why won't your AI confirm this?" Gage asked.

"Grynau—my AI—has the succession list," Thorvald said. "You must be on it, as Grynau recognized you as regent over Lady Christina, whose familial relationship to the King is well-known. But…I'm not Captain Royce. I bonded improperly to the AI and much is locked away from me. If you doubt what I'm telling you, have Dr. Seaver confirm it."

"Won't Salis' armor stop that if the boy isn't injured? Designer viruses and—"

Thorvald reached into a pocket and removed a small plastic bag with a single square of the shiftable armor he once wore and tossed it onto the desk. Dried blood smudged an edge.

"You broke with your suit to tell me this," Gage said.

"Yes, sire."

"And you know what it means? Nothing, Thorvald. This doesn't change anything."

"But as King, you can—"

"Do what?" Gage asked, standing and raising his arms. "I am the Commodore. I command this fleet and every Albion military member until such time as we find an admiral—one that isn't coopted by the Daegon—and I turn over command. Not that there's much chance of that happening. I'm regent by my rank and Aidan's age, which makes me head of state."

"Not to the League," Thorvald said. "I was there. I saw—"

"That was not the League!" Gage slammed a hand to the desk. "They were not heads of state. They were scared bureaucrats too timid to make any real decisions. There was no leadership in that room. We have to deal with these…with whatever happened to the 5th Fleet and return to Lantau with our heads high. With a clear purpose. Albion carries the torch, Thorvald. Her light turns back the darkness and I…"

Gage trailed off and went to a window where

stars streaked by as the ship moved through slip space.

"We believe things about ourselves," Gage said. "We have these ideas…of how things should be. Now I learn that the man I thought was my father isn't and my real father…" He shook his head. "It was bad enough to be a common-born officer trying to lead this fleet. If I make this known, then what?"

"The fleet will believe you," Thorvald said. "There's evidence."

"They'll believe I'm a pretender," Gage said. "Remember all the jokes that went around after Francia fell to the Reich? Every last officer with a few ships or soldiers under their command declared themselves the one true Dauphin. They fled into wild space to set up 'governments in exile' and degenerated into pirates within a few years."

"This isn't—"

"No, which is why I went to the League to bring them into the fight to free Albion. The Reich conquered Francia, occupied their worlds, but their people still survive. Their way of life is still there, even if it's under the Reich's rule. The Daegon are different, Thorvald. They will erase everything we are and make us slaves. I must save Albion quickly before there's nothing left to save."

"Spoken like a true King," Thorvald said.

"No…spoken like any man of Albion. But I can't do this as King. If I try and take the crown from Aidan, I'll be labeled an opportunist. A usurper. The truth doesn't matter when so many can believe an easy lie. My parentage can never leave this room, Thorvald."

"I lived amongst your people for almost two decades," the Genevan said. "They will rally around you. No more dissent like Arlyss."

"Arlyss is a coward and a fool," Gage said. "The rest of the commanders have a lick of sense to them. You tell no one else. Understood?"

"But—"

"I don't want it, Thorvald. I can keep saying that over and over, but I don't need you to understand that…just obey. Obey me as the King or as regent to your last dying breath. The difference doesn't matter to me, because if somehow the fleet learns of this, I'll deny it all."

"I will obey you," Thorvald said.

"Now go get your armor back on. We'll be at Basai soon."

"That…won't be possible," Thorvald said. "Grynau will not accept me after this. First, I betrayed my oaths and put the palace in danger…then I broke from my House again to tell you the truth. You are everything Albion should be, while I am a failure to Geneva."

"Then your suit is…"

Thorvald went to the door to the wardroom and it slid open. The armor stood just outside, the back of one arm visible to Gage from where it stood guard.

"The AI still has its mission," Thorvald said. "It will protect you as best it can, but it may be erratic."

"I can't have a haunted suit following me around." Gage rubbed the bridge of his nose. "Take it to Aidan's quarters and post it on guard there."

"Then I will—"

"No," Gage said. "You're erratic, Thorvald. Your decisions aren't helping me, Aidan, or Albion.

Report to Salis. She's head of the protection detail now. I'll make up my mind as to what to do with you after we return to Lantau."

Thorvald took a step toward Gage and the armor leaned around to look into the wardroom.

"Yes, sire." Thorvald's face fell. "As you wish."

"Go."

Thorvald walked out and the armor followed him down the passageway.

Gage keyed the door shut and opened a desk drawer. He took out a scuffed data slate and swiped through to a picture of his mother and the man he once believed was his father on their wedding day. He looked at a painting of King Randolph on the wall and held up the slate, comparing the likeness between the King and his mother, then he tossed the slate onto the desk and ran his hand along his chin.

He'd had facial reconstructive surgery as a child. He remembered his mother calming him before the procedure…telling him he'd been in an accident. But in the years after that and before her suicide, she never explained what that accident had been.

"All a lie," he said. "All of it was a lie. But if I'd known the truth…where would I be now?"

Gage picked up a different slate and watched as new messages came in with ship-ready reports, logistics projections and a flashing timer counting down to the fleet's arrival at Basai.

"King or regent…doesn't change the problem right in front of me. My title doesn't matter. Only my duties," Gage muttered as he sat down and went to work.

Chapter 12

What had once been a Concord National Guard armory had been converted into a fortress. Rows of razor wire clogged the street leading up to the building, though they were pockmarked by shell craters, a crashed Daegon fighter, and fragments of the multi-storey buildings surrounding the armory.

Seaver glanced over a half-collapsed wall. The armory was a few hundred yards away, and a bullet-torn and dirty flag hung from the walls that were edged with spikes, each of which was topped with a head. Some still wore their Daegon helmets; others had normal human skin tones, but he glanced at a few with the invaders' green and purple hues.

A bullet struck just to one side of his face and

everything went white as pulverized masonry covered his visor. Seaver fell back and tripped over a brick, landing clumsily on his rear end.

Juliae knelt against the wall, seemingly unconcerned.

"Same sniper?" Powell asked.

"Hell if I know." Seaver brushed dirt off his face, then raised the bottom of his helmet to spit. "I can't tell if the bastard's a good shot for almost hitting me from where he's at, or a lousy shot because he keeps missing."

"Stop giving him chances," Powell said. "I don't want to hump all your gear out of here," she added, kicking a bag full of Inez's armor. They'd stripped his corpse clean back in the school and left his body behind. Juliae said the resources that had gone into his equipment were too valuable for the Concordians to find.

"Fine by me," Seaver said.

"Covering fire," Juliae said, pointing to a mound of rubble leading up to a gap in the roof. "We attack."

"Centurion, that's…" Seaver was about to

point out that infantry assaulting a fortified position without armor or artillery support was tantamount to suicide. But one look from Juliae quelled his protest. She knew as well as he did.

He just didn't know if she cared.

"Covering fire, yes, Master." Seaver went to the base of the rubble and tested a foothold.

A whistle blew, and a battle cry rose up all around Seaver. He rushed up the slope, bringing his machine gun up to his shoulder.

Black-clad themata rushed toward the Concord strongpoint as muzzle flashes broke out from surrounding buildings and bunkers in the armory. Seaver opened fire, targeting the small slit where the defenders had a belt-fed machine gun like his.

Themata went down quickly, shot as they struggled through razor wire and tripped over their own dead.

"No, no, they're Albion," Seaver muttered as he shifted his fire from the bunker and raked bullets across the upper wall where defenders were firing. One bullet hit one of the two ropes securing the flag to the battlements and a corner slumped down.

He knocked out an empty magazine and slapped in a new one, his barrel glowing hot.

A defender leaned over the wall and grasped at the flag, catching an edge in his hand.

Seaver aimed carefully and hit the soldier in the back. He jerked and fell over the wall, ripping the flag down with him and leaving a bloody splatter as a testament to Seaver's marksmanship.

A bullet crashed into his machine gun breach and ricocheted up and into his chest, punching him off his feet and sending him rolling down the debris pile to the ground. He tried to breathe, but his lungs refused to work with him. Rolling onto his back, he touched his breastplate. It was cracked, but there was no blood.

Managing a halting gasp, he rolled to his side as Juliae looked at him, then shook her head slowly.

He found his machine gun, the carriage and breach bent and broken by the sniper's bullet. Useless.

Three quick whistle blows snapped his head up and he looked for a way out of the room. Three whistles was the signal to retreat, one of the many simple battlefield commands Keoni had drilled into him and the rest of the themata during their transit to Concord.

"Stay." Juliae tossed him Inez's machine gun and waved Powell over to the ammo pile. Powell turned around and Juliae pressed new magazines into empty mag locks on her back. "Our attack was reconnaissance."

Seaver felt a rumble through the ground, as if cattle were stampeding and bearing down on him. Outside the building, golems charged toward the armory and Daegon fighters roared overhead.

The crash of rockets exploding reverberated through the city and the slow chug of the golems' weapons made the sound of his own machine gun sound like a child's toy in comparison.

"Forward." Juliae swept out through a gap in the wall and Seaver and Powell followed her, keeping low as she worked her way through a wrecked building to find Keoni. The legio was kicking a themata on the ground.

Shell-shocked, bloody soldiers clung to what

cover they could find, none seeming to care why Keoni was beating the other one.

"Coward. You get up and die with everyone!" Keoni landed a kick in the man's groin and he whined in pain.

Noticing a bloody gunshot wound on the man's thigh, Seaver said, "Legio," and brushed his hand across his own leg.

"Huh?" Keoni stopped the beating and locked the shock maul to his lower back. "You were hit?"

"Yes, Legio!" the man gasped.

"Can you fight?" Keoni asked.

"No, Legio. I can't walk. Can't—"

Keoni grabbed him by the top of his head and the pneumatic spike crushed the wounded man's skull.

"How many still effective?" Juliae asked.

"Maybe…nineteen," the legio said. "More out there, but no last long."

Seaver looked around a low wall and watched as the golems advanced, never slowing their march forward or their rate of fire. The heavy-caliber bullets had eaten away at all the bunkers, chipping through all the concrete and steel and leaving them open and exposed like fruit picked apart by birds.

At the back of the advance, golems shot out windows, methodically reducing each Concord strongpoint surrounding the armory.

They used us to draw out all the enemy's fire, Seaver thought. *Our lives spent to make the next attack more effective.*

There was a thunderclap and the leading golem exploded, its head shooting up and arcing down, slamming to the ground between Seaver and Juliae. The helmet spun around, internal circuits sparking. Inside was nothing—no sign of the person he thought was in the golem, not even a hint of blood.

A tank rolled out around the armory and fired on the golems again, destroying two with one shell.

"Live free or die!"

Seaver heard the battle cry as more golems went down.

"Tanks sighted," Juliae said, one hand to the side of her helmet. "Counterattack. I say again, local counterattack, vicinity key terrain epsilon seven...What? No. We're too close. Give us—whore sons!"

Juliae pinched the chin of her helmet and Seaver's own suit tightened. His airflow cut off for a moment, then stale air with a hint of iodine flooded around his face.

"Legio..." Juliae waved an arm up and away from the fortress. "Pull back. Leave the wounded. Pull back—*ventus rutilus*."

"Run!" Keoni grabbed a themata and shoved him up and away from the battle where the golems were being forced back by more Concord tanks.

"Contact," Seaver said, hefting up his new machine gun. "Enemy infantry coming out of the target building." He struggled to breathe, the airflow inside his helmet too little for what his lungs needed.

"I say run!" Keoni hit a slow themata across the back of his legs with his unpowered shock maul and cut past Juliae and her two shaped bodyguards. The Daegon stayed in place, urging her themata away and pointing where to go.

A Daegon fighter snapped overhead, and

thick red contrails arced down from the flight path. A smoking canister bounced off the armory wall near the blood splatter from Seaver's last kill, and a deep-crimson wave billowed out, washing over the Concord soldiers and their tanks.

An eerie silence fell over the battlefield as more clouds grew up and around the armory. Seaver inched backwards as the red bore down on him, but Juliae walked out into the open and held her hands to her sides as it washed over them all.

The sky went pink and red air pooled across the ground.

From behind Seaver came a horrible retch. One of the themata was on the ground, the blood from a compound fracture in his ankle staining his boot. The themata hacked and a glob of blood splattered beneath his face.

"Let me help," Seaver said, grabbing him beneath one arm and lifting him up.

The themata turned around. Blood poured from his eyeballs. Fluid leaked out his nose and mouth, and he hacked again, coughing up a disgusting mass onto Seaver's chest. The man collapsed, his limbs twitching as a seizure took hold of his entire body.

Juliae pushed Seaver to one side and put her boot heel to the dying man's neck. She snapped his vertebrae with a quick twist, but the body kept twitching.

"Finish off any more of ours you find," she said. "The *ventus rutilus* is a slow death…but it is a sure death."

"It's on us," Powell said. "It's all over us. What if we—"

"It won't last long. Just don't breathe it," Juliae said. "Nicias wants us at a staging point. Come." She made a simple gesture to follow.

Seaver looked back at the armory. The only sound of fighting he heard was from the golems' weapons. How many people lay dead in the red mist? He pointed back and saw corrosion eating at the edges of his plates.

"Powell," he said.

"I know. To hell with the rest of them. Stay with Juliae." She stepped over the dead man and hurried after the Daegon.

Hacks and the moans of the dying carried through the mist as Seaver went after his charge, brushing off the edge of his armor as best he could.

Chapter 13

Steam washed over Seaver as he walked through a decontamination station. He passed through and took his machine gun from Powell. The corrosion on their armor made them look like they'd been fighting for years on end, not the mere hours spent on Concord.

At least he thought it was hours. Time had become a blur since the crash landing.

The Daegon staging point was a loose perimeter around a cargo lander. Slaves with exoskeletons bolted to their bodies moved ammo crates and other gear into clusters around the lander.

An old man with sun-damaged skin motioned them toward a group of women holding pressure washers and brushes.

"All stations," he said in thickly accented Daegon. "Each. Each."

"There's food," Powell said, pointing farther down the ring.

"You hungry?" Seaver asked, going to the first point and mimicking the T-pose one of the slave women made. She and others sprayed his armor and scrubbed him down, while an old woman spritzed a cloth and rubbed his face with a fair degree of gentleness.

"Go. Next." She slapped him on the rear end and he and Powell went to the next station, where a robot took their machine guns and small servo arms popped out of its back to service their weapons.

"I'm not hungry, but I could eat," Seaver said. "Who knows when we'll get the chance to do that again." He looked over his armor, which had been scoured of the corrosion and looked almost brand-new.

"I'm…calm. So calm it bothers me here," she touched her temple, then her chest, "but not here."

"I know that feeling…or not-feeling. Must be

whatever the Daegon did to us," he said. "Easier if you think about it. Imagine trying to process all that back there." He jerked a thumb over his shoulder.

"Must be why they shaped us." Powell ran a hand down her distended jaw. "I'm hideous now, aren't I?"

"Does it matter? We wear a full-faced helmet when we fight," he said.

"Ass." She got a fresh resupply of ammo from the next station, then they went to a small kitchen. A group of other shaped soldiers stood around tall tables, plates of food and foam cups in front of them.

Seaver got a steaming pile of the same ground-up meat he'd had when he woke up after his transformation and a cup of pale-white liquid. As they went to an unoccupied end of a table, none of the other shapes seemed to care about their arrival.

"This mush is my new favorite," Powell said, scooping a spoonful into her mouth and chewing loudly before swallowing. "That's the plan for when this ends. Mush Express. Best mush restaurant this side of the Great Veil."

Seaver took a sip of the drink. It was bitter and tasted of electrolytes.

"Shrimp mush. Habanero mush. Maybe you can freeze it and put it on a stick. Dessert mush," Powell mumbled between bites.

"Oye." Another shaped came over and dropped his plate next to Seaver's. The new arrival's skin was sallow, his eyes and cheeks sunken. His body was still impressively large, but he looked like he was on death's door.

"Oye, you two know my bro?" He touched the sigil on his chest, then pointed at Seaver's. "Keoni. From Papa'apoho like me."

"He's our legio, master," Powell said.

"No 'master.'" The shaped chuckled. "Just a twist like you. Keoni get hurt stick and think he all that? That Keoni. He alive still?"

"Yes," Seaver said. "He's with what's left of our themata."

"Knew it. You tell him Pika didn't forget bet. Pika still alive. For bit more." The shaped took a bite and chewed slowly, as if it gave him pain.

"How long…have you been…" Powell

motioned to her face.

"Six month." Pika pushed the lip of his cup against the side of his mouth and tilted his head back to drink. "Six month. I tough. Good centurion send me to *ali'i kane* medicine. Most us last three month. Or enemy end sooner." He smiled with only one half of his mouth. The rest didn't seem to move.

"Three months?" Powell dropped her spoon.

"Want to serve Daegon longer? Go be a tiki," Pika said.

Seaver concentrated on finishing his food, as the other shaped had no interest in conversation. A tightening at his neck pulled him away before he finished; Juliae needed him. Powell and he dumped their trays in a bin and went to the center of the resupply point, where they waited at the base of the shuttle's ramp. Daegon warriors stood around an officer with a short white cape, Juliae at the outer edge.

The Daegon saluted and came down the ramp. Seaver and Powell fell in behind their centurion as she moved at a brisk pace toward the front, where the bomb of artillery and steady rumble of aircraft continued.

"The final battle is at hand," Juliae said. "Nicias is ready to take the Hexen."

"Our themata?" Seaver asked.

"Nicias—in his wisdom—has ordered all themata not on the front lines back to the logistics fields to serve as labor. That makes me something of a lance corporal and we've been assigned to Triarii Isaac for the duration. A Daegon and shaped cohort. You two will keep up with me," she said.

"Yes, master," Seaver said. The sound of battle grew as they neared the front lines.

****

Seaver swept his muzzle around a corner to a dark living room. The house was still largely intact in this upscale neighborhood. Picture frames were askew and stray rounds had punched holes in the wall and wrecked one liquor cabinet, but otherwise, it was tidy.

"Room clear," Seaver said and the torque around his neck tightened slightly as Juliae acknowledged.

He swung the infrared light on his machine gun—it being just past dusk and a white light was a sure way to attract attention from that damned sniper (if he was still alive)—and froze.

Several pairs of feet stuck out from behind a couch. Their reading was cool, almost room temperature. Dead for some time, but dead recently. He didn't move as his eyes locked on two small pairs of feet mixed in with adults'.

"Suicide or murder?" Juliae asked from behind him.

He whirled around, almost drawing down on her, but he jerked his muzzle back.

"Others report the same thing." She opened a kitchen cabinet and plucked out a plate of fine china. "Entire families dead in mass poisonings. Such a waste, isn't it? Not uncommon through the course of history when all hope is lost for a people. All we demand is submission to our enlightened rule, the same rule that guided humanity for millennia. There's peace in submission, no need to fear the consequences when agency is gone. The Daegon will return all of humanity to that right and proper time.

They'll learn. They'll all learn in time."

"Master, forgive me, but…I don't understand what you mean," Seaver said.

"Obedience first, comprehension later. The good slave learns to love the lash…in time." She spun the plate around and set it gently onto a countertop. "I understand why you don't recognize us. We had to leave you ferals behind to save the future. Then our promised Eden turned into something else entirely. But our struggle gave us more than a skin color to set us apart from you all…it made us better. Centuries living on the edge of extinction…but we prevailed. Tell me, shaped, who ruled humanity before the Edziza eruption?"

"That was almost a thousand years ago, but…there were a lot of different countries on Earth back then. Mars was its own colony. Luna too. The people—"

"No!" Juliae beat a fist against the plate and shattered it across the counter. "No, Earth was ruled by us. We let the peasants and the 'common man' have the illusion of self-determination, but it was all under our control. The governments. Media. Banks.

All of it was ours. We lost some power in the late eighteenth century, but it was all ours again for a glorious time before the catastrophe. The wars stopped. 'Freedom'—if there is such a thing—ended. All was glorious fealty to the families. We'll rule again. You'll see."

"They didn't see it that way," Seaver said, motioning to the dead. "Not everyone in settled space will."

"Albion has bent the knee," she said. "If your world can submit, all worlds can submit…or be destroyed like this one. The Triarii found and killed the team that was harassing our supply lines. The Hexen awaits."

There was a crash of breaking glass from a window and Powell dropped down from the second floor to outside the kitchen.

"A senator or something like that lived here," she said as Juliae and Seaver left out the back. "Expensive stuff in the bedroom. Fancy clothes in the closet, big old sash with medals and such."

"Good that he saved us the trouble of having to kill him," Juliae said. "We do not let feral leaders survive…unless parading them about as slaves serves our purpose better."

Seaver felt a tinge of true anger at that. Word among the Albion resistance was that Prince Aidan had made it off world. So long as the Prince lived, then Albion was not truly conquered. The star nation had always been known for its fierce independence…though not as extreme as Concord and its refusal to act beyond its system. Yet now here were Albion soldiers sent to subjugate this world. He suspected the Daegon commander knew exactly what he was doing when he sent the Albion thematas to fight here.

"This will be interesting." Juliae cut through a fire-swept forest and to a football field where three war machines sat on the melted fake grass.

Seaver almost tripped when he realized they were walkers. An armored chassis—with a central energy lance and several machine guns covering all angles of the machine—sat between three bent legs to keep their profile low. He wasn't sure which had been a worse fight back on Albion—the golems seemed to take pleasure in ripping his fellow soldiers apart, but the walkers had a penchant for annihilating entire buildings where they encountered resistance.

Other Daegon soldiers and their shaped—one had five in his retinue—milled about the soccer field.

"We're to keep pace with them," Juliae said. "They're vulnerable from below. Keep the ferals from sneaking too near and hitting them with rockets. Don't chase them down. They've managed to successfully bird-dog our infantry away a few times, though there have been more reports of suicide attacks as we get closer to the Hexen."

"Are we going in there?" Powell motioned to the capitol building, lit up by flames. Smoke rose into the night sky as tracer fire from air defense cannons reached after passing Daegon fighters.

"Likely not." Juliae shrugged. "Walkers will get close enough, reduce the structure. Then golems will be sent through what remains. But if we're ordered inside…leave the final bunker to Daegon. Their leadership demands personal attention from us."

A whine rose from the walkers and the clawed feet of the legs gripped hard. The chassis rose up and the three moved toward the Hexen. Juliae ran through the stomping legs, dancing around them like a cat maneuvering beneath a table.

Seaver followed as fast as he could, praying that he wouldn't get stepped on and be responsible for his father's death because he died in such a stupid, useless manner.

They stayed a block ahead of the walkers as they made their way through the upscale neighborhood. Dead dogs, civilians, and soldiers lay in the streets. Most had a red pallor, victims of the same gas the Daegon had used at the armory.

"Taking them out from orbit would have been kinder," Powell said.

"Silence," Juliae hissed. "They were warned."

Seaver went to one knee next to a ground car that had crashed into a low wall with the name of the neighborhood carved into it. A radio crackled from within, the driver and his passenger slumped over and dead. He wasn't sure if the crash or the gas had done them in.

"Concord Concord. This is Reverend Paul with a final message," came from the dashboard. "In our final hours. Do not despair. Our Lord demanded we be free, and to die free men is His will. Heaven awaits those that live and died to His word and His command. Do not despair. Fight on to the last. Concord Concord. This is Reverend Paul with a final message…"

"Master, do you hear this?" Seaver asked.

"Let them pray to whatever god they think is there," the Daegon said, waving a hand dismissively. "We don't care."

They came down a hill and passed a casualty collection point. Slaves in gray tunics pawed through the bodies of dead themata, moving their weapons and gear into piles before tossing the bodies into mass graves.

The front line was a mess of small fires and scattered pockets of Daegon troops. Juliae moved through them all effortlessly, without any fear of being shot by a spooked, exhausted themata infantryman. More centurions spread out around her, their shaped struggling to keep up.

"What did they do to her?" Powell asked Seaver. "She's…she's natural, right? Not some shake-

and-bake roid freak like us."

"Don't know." Seaver ducked as a burst of rifle fire sounded in the distance. "Don't care right now. Just keep up."

The walkers followed and the themata cheered when the telephone-pole-like legs stomped down in the middle of their positions. More than one was nearly crushed as the walkers paid no heed to the slave soldiers' safety.

"The Hexen's shields are still up," Juliae said through their internal comms. "The walkers need to get closer…and there's some strange reports from the forward lines. We're to clear it out."

Seaver brushed past a ground car. The entire vehicle had a red dusting and the sidewalk next to it bore tracks from passing soldiers. Another shaped had assured Seaver that the *ventus rutilus* ceased being lethal within minutes of being employed, but he opted to stay in the tracks and brushed off the dust when he noticed it on his arms and weapon.

Juliae slid to a stop against a wall of a tavern, the carved wooden sign hanging from one hinge and swaying gently. Seaver and Powell came to either side of her, scanning windows and a half-full parking lot for any movement. Lights were still on across the city, but it had gone eerily silent.

"This place is a graveyard," Powell said.

"The ferals pulled back to deal with our attack from the east, left themselves wide open here," Juliae said. "But our infantry in this sector just went dark…Seaver, one on foot. Stop him." She tapped the side of her helmet then pointed to the edge of the building.

Seaver shuffled over, hearing the stomp of someone running growing stronger. He waited a moment, then reached out and caught a themata by the waist, yanking him off the sidewalk.

"No! The *bawbach*! The *bawbach* are right behind me!" The themata squirmed in Seaver's grasp and clawed at the ground.

"The what?" Seaver grabbed the themata by the back of his shirt, but the man flipped around and slipped away, leaving Seaver holding his top. Seaver, without even thinking, aimed his machine gun at the fleeing soldier.

"Leave him," Juliae said. "A legio will deal

with it. Don't give our position away."

"Yes, master." Seaver paused and looked at the weapon in his hands. Was he really going to shoot him?

"A *bawbach*," Powell said. "That's an old wives' tale from around Ferndale. Near where I grew up on Albion. Dead come back to haunt the living."

"Ridiculous," Juliae said. "Stress or simple cowardice. I'll find his torque and kill him now."

Seaver looked up the street, then did a double take.

A man in a khaki Concord uniform stood on a corner, a white cloth tied over his lower face, a streak of red smeared down the center from his mouth and nose. He swung a rifle with a bayonet to one side and charged at Seaver.

More soldiers appeared from buildings and behind cars, all with sheets or scraps of uniforms wrapped around their nose and jaws. All run through with blood.

They ran forward with a low war cry that gurgled in ruined throats.

"Contact!" Seaver called, backing down the

sidewalk and fumbling with his weapon as the dozens of soldiers came for him. "Contact!"

He shot down the closest—two hits to the upper chest that pitched the man back and folded him at the knees—then he opened up at full auto, sweeping fire back and forth at the wave of bloody attackers until he was hit from the side in the knees and flank, sending him stumbling down and losing his hold on his weapon.

A Concord soldier came face-to-face with him. The soldier's mouth was a red and black maw, his once-white covering dangling from his neck. One eye had burst, leaving a sticky smear down the side of his face, and a blood droplet spattered across Seaver's faceplate as the soldier thrust a knife at his neck.

Despite all the Daegon had done to his body and mind when they shaped him, genuine terror gripped Seaver now, freezing him in place as this dead man tried to kill him. The blade scraped against the top of his breastplate and the soldier's strike went past Seaver's head.

Seaver grabbed him by the throat, the feel of slick, hot blood awakening some atavistic reaction in his mind, and he squeezed hard. The soldier's neck snapped, and his mouth popped open, rivulets of blood stretching down toward Seaver's face.

He screamed and flung the corpse against a nearby car then sat up just as more of the bloody, gasping Concord soldiers charged at him, bayonets ready. One raised his rifle and thrust at his heart.

Seaver slapped the rifle to one side, but the blade caught against his other arm and pierced through the chain mail beneath his armor plate. It got caught in his bicep and a dull pain jolted his body. Seaver rolled toward the rifle and twisted it out of the soldier's grasp. He yanked the bayonet out of his arm and slashed the same blade across the Concord man's throat, cutting down to the spine and killing him.

A Daegon machine gun opened fire and Powell cut down the ghastly soldiers trying to swarm Seaver. He hacked at them with the one arm holding the rifle as bullets punched the soldiers off their feet. They fell without a sound, almost like they were fighting ghosts.

Seaver looked back and found Juliae with one hand to her helmet, dead Concordians at her feet. A soldier with blood-soaked checkered tablecloth around his face rose up from the roof of the tavern, a stick grenade in hand. He pulled the pin and raised it, ready to throw it at the unsuspecting Daegon.

Seaver reversed the grip on his rifle and threw it like a spear. The bayonet caught the soldier in the chest and he dropped the grenade.

"Master!" Seaver sprinted forward and tackled Juliae, covering her as the grenade exploded and wrecked the tavern's roof.

Seaver's chin lifted, Juliae's pistol pushing it up until Seaver rolled off.

Powell's magazine ran empty and she swung her machine gun like a club, crushing Concordians with each swing.

"Do something useful!" Juliae smacked him on the side of the head and opened fire with her pistol.

Seaver's left arm refused to bend, but he got to his feet and ran back to Powell. He shoulder-checked a soldier off his feet, sending the man headfirst into a car window so hard, he exploded out of the windshield and onto the street.

Seaver punched a soldier in the face, grabbed him by the blood-soaked shirt, and tossed him into the legs of three more Concordians coming for him. Dozens more were on the street, all determined to kill the Daegon and her protectors.

"Drop," Powell snapped.

Seaver went prone, a smile on his face as she opened fire. He'd bought her just enough time to reload. The *tat-tat-tat* of her weapon grew louder, echoing through the city and overlapping. As he crawled to his own machine gun, shell casings rained down around him.

He rolled over and looked up at a walker. Guns blazed from each bottom corner and a ball turret underneath swept back and forth, chain guns tracing nearly continuous lines as it annihilated the attacking Concordians.

Seaver stood up, dragging the barrel of his machine gun across the ground as he rose. Blood ran down one arm and dripped from his fingers, and he stopped to consider just how badly hurt he really was.

When he noticed a red mist hanging in the air, he began to panic, fearing the Daegon had used their gas weapon again. But it wasn't the *ventus rutilus*. It was blood from the street full of dead Concord soldiers. The walker's high-velocity rounds had popped the defenders like balloons, leaving a trail of gore up the street.

Seaver dropped his weapon, the hellscape before him overwhelming his conditioning.

"You. Here." Juliae pulled him out of the way as the walker stomped forward. A needle popped out over one finger and she stuck it into the port on his collarbone.

Seaver gasped as a rush of energy filled him, his heart beating so hard, his breastplate quivered.

Juliae took a small vial off her belt and sprayed his wounded arm. Pink foam covered the injury and the bleeding ceased.

"What's happening?" Powell put both hands against her helmet and tried to push it off. "Why did they…they were already dead. Already dead!"

Juliae held up a hand, her fingers bent to some arcane symbol, and Powell slumped to her knees.

"Your shaping wasn't complete," Juliae said.

"I brought you to this battle too soon. Your bodies can't take the stress or the chemicals." She grabbed Seaver by the side of his helmet and turned his head toward hers. Popping her visor up, she looked him in the eyes.

"You're going to be OK," she said, and Seaver dreamed that there was actual concern behind her eyes. "If you lose control, I will put you down without hesitation, you get that?"

"Yes…Julie. Eye." Seaver wobbled, and she had to keep him on his feet.

A sheen of light grew in the distance and his head cleared slightly.

"Ah…the end begins," Juliae said. "Shield flare from the walker's plasma cannons striking the Hexen." She took her hand away from Seaver and waited to see if he could stand on his own. "You're doing better. Help the other. I want to take this moment in."

The Daegon climbed up the broken wall wrecked by the grenade earlier and peeked just over the roof toward the capitol building.

"Sniper," Seaver managed, reaching for her.

"The walker has overwatch," she said, waving him off. "The other."

Seaver lurched over to Powell, who'd gone back to trying to get her helmet off. Seaver touched the release on the back of her head and the helmet came up and bounced off her thighs. Powell gasped like she'd just come up for air after a deep dive, a sheen of sweat glistening in the streetlights.

"Couldn't…breathe," she said.

"Yes, you can." Seaver put his good arm around her shoulders. "We're going to make it. Just keep breathing."

"I…want…to go…home," she said between gulps of air.

An explosion rumbled in the distance.

"Their shields are down!" Juliae slapped the wall in excitement. "Come watch! Come watch!"

"What're we doing?" Powell asked quietly. "What're we turning into?"

"Just get through today," Seaver said, giving her helmet back. She struggled to get it back on.

A dull-yellow light grew from the walker's plasma cannon, a new star forming in the sky.

"Here we go!" Juliae shouted.

There was a sudden flash and an intense heat enveloped him as a blast wave knocked him flat and sent him skidding into the next building and through the wall. A tsunami of rushing air passed over him, his hearing degraded into a dull whine as he lay stunned, his mind a blank as he struggled to process what had just transpired.

Seaver tested his limbs—a dull pain down his right side, his left arm still refusing to bend. A red glare shone through gaps in the wall that had collapsed on top of him. He knocked bricks away, thankful for the helmet and armor that just saved his life. He looked up and watched an atomic fireball rise from where the Hexen had been and scorch the sky.

Black rain spattered against his visor.

"Powell? Centurion?" Seaver pulled himself out of the rubble. All color had been burned out of the city. The red dust was gone, replaced with a scab of white over the buildings and cars. A walker leg lay in the street, sparks crackling from the joints.

His HUD fritzed on and off as the rain grew harder, each drop burning like acid against his armor.

"Anybody?" Seaver spied an armored foot sticking out from beneath a car tilted up against the same building he'd hit. He grabbed the car by the bumper and pulled it down, rain lashing at him as he came around.

A hunk of wood had impaled Powell through the chest. One hand was on the jagged edge, her eyes dead and staring at the sky.

"Ah…no. What do I…where's the…" Seaver's HUD went into a static haze and he tossed his helmet aside. The black rain struck his face and dribbled into his mouth. He spat it out, ignoring the almost electric taste to it, and looked around.

The city smoldered like old ashes. The patter of fallout sounded like a spring rain back home and he couldn't see anything or anyone moving.

"Am I…dead?" He looked up to the sky…and saw a Daegon fighter cross beneath clouds lit up by the fireball. "No…not dead yet."

A groan rose from somewhere nearby.

"Centurion?" Seaver stumbled through the collapsed building and found a hand sticking up from the rubble. Using his good arm, he knocked away broken bricks and found Juliae.

The armor of her head and shoulders was scorched; heat bubbles pulsated off the metal. A smell of burnt hair and cooking meat assaulted Seaver's nose.

Juliae pawed at her ruined helmet and Seaver swallowed hard. He flipped the latch on the back of her helmet and her visor popped free. He lifted it up, feeling something catch beneath it.

The Daegon growled in pain, the flesh over her left eye and cheek badly burned. Her veins pulsed black and one eye glared at him.

"The radiation," she hissed. "I can't…can't take the rads. Get me back…get me out of here. Now!"

Seaver breathed faster. The urge to strangle her was almost palpable. There was no one to stop him. No one to witness it. If they both died out here now…the Daegon wouldn't punish his father…would they?

"Help," Juliae gasped, and fear—an actual emotion—crossed her face. "Help me, Seaver."

The urge to kill faded away, and he dug her

out. The burns to her face were the only injuries he could find, but the darkness in her veins grew deeper as time passed.

"Our doctors," she said, her words catching in her throat like she was on the verge of an asthma attack. "Get me to my doctor. They...know what..."

Seaver put her arm over his shoulder and lifted her up. He bent down and she fell across his shoulders. He strained as he lifted her up and started walking back to the Daegon lines.

He focused on putting one foot in front of the other as his gums began to bleed and a taste of iron filled his mouth.

Chapter 14

Fractal patterns danced across Tolan's vision, a wooden pipe slipping out of his hands and rattling against the deck as he drifted back. The mix of whatever he'd bought from the drug dealer aboard the station wasn't as advertised, but he was loving the effects. The feel of needle stings against his feet was a bit distressing, but he concentrated on the trip as the sound of a woman's laughter rose in his ears.

The laugh morphed into a high-pitched *ree ree* over and over and a worry grew in the back of his mind. The sound was familiar…almost like an alarm.

Tolan sat up and looked at his control panel. One button pulsed on and off, and his drug-induced haze made the rest of his control panel light up light a

Christmas tree.

"Whoa…neat." Tolan blinked hard.

A drum beat behind him, and he was about to get up to dance when he realized it was Loussan banging against the bridge door. Reaching under the console, Tolan grabbed a pistol, then pulled a lever to unlock the door.

"Don't you…harsh me," Tolan slurred. Loussan plucked the pistol out of his hand and answered the hail that had been coming in.

"Novis regiray," a harsh voice said and Tolan tried to tickle Loussan.

"This is the freighter *Cassio*," Loussan said. "How may we be of service?"

"Transmit all technical data for your ship. Now," said the Daegon on the other end of the hail. "State your cargo."

"Holds are empty." Loussan tucked the pistol into the back of his pants and tapped a keypad. When an access command came up, he mashed Tolan's hand against a biometric reader as the spy blew a raspberry. "Sending specs now."

Loussan hit mute and slapped Tolan away as

he fumbled for the weapon and inadvertently pinched Loussan's rear.

"I will slap you sober if you don't get yourself under control," Loussan hissed.

"Harsh," Tolan pouted and crossed his arms over his chest.

"Freighter *Cassio*," the Daegon said, "your slip engine lists best speed as factor nine. Is that correct?"

Loussan looked at Tolan, who warbled as he gyrated a finger across his lips. Loussan slapped a hand over Tolan's mouth.

"Factor nine, confirmed," Loussan said.

"Stand by for inspection." The channel cut out.

"Shit!" Loussan slapped at Tolan's robes, eliciting a giggle from the spy. "They're coming, you goddamn addict. This might be our ticket out of here and you're…what are you on?"

Tolan closed his eyes hard, then popped them open. "Leather case," he said, jerking a thumb over his shoulder then turning his seat around to point his thumb at a locker.

"If this was my ship, I'd throw you out the

nearest air lock at my earliest convenience. My crew knew when to indulge—" he said as he flung the locker open and hefted out a briefcase, "—and when to stay sharp. The Daegon will be here any minute and—" he popped the case open, "—fuck me sideways…"

Inside were racks of vials, dozens of pill cases, a brass hypodermic set, several vacuum-sealed packs of dried fungi…and one with neon-blue worms.

"I'm a collector." Tolan waggled his eyebrows at Loussan. "Give me compound L-C-37. Green glass. Red cap."

"That will sober you up?" Loussan asked.

Tolan frowned and his head shifted from side to side. "Yes…yes."

"I'm going to dump all this in the incinerator when I have the chance," Loussan said, tapping vials and pulling out one that matched Tolan's description. A green gas swirled within.

"Gimmee…you harsher." Tolan took the vial and tried to open it, but his hand slipped off the cap and the vial flipped up into the air.

"I hate you jackboots," Loussan muttered as

he twisted the cap off and jammed it beneath Tolan's nose. Tolan snorted and went rigid. Loussan wrinkled his nose at the stench from the vial and closed it.

The spy hunched forward, gripping his stomach and letting out an ugly groan.

"I hope this hurts and you learn a lesson," Loussan said.

Tolan's hair changed. The thin brown hair thickened into black curls. His ears went limp and flopped down next to his face. Tolan raised his head slowly and Loussan jumped back.

The spy's face had lost all elasticity and draped down from his cheeks, jowls, and eyes like he was melting. One iris changed from red to black to green, then went pale as a cataract. Tolan caught the edge of his loose skin and mashed it back against his face, leaving an imprint of his hand over his mouth and nose.

"Flababa," Tolan said, pointing at the case as his fingers lengthened unevenly with the crack of bones.

"Did I…do I have a contact high?" Loussan looked at the green vial in his hand.

Tolan pressed his drooping lips against his teeth.

"Hypoderm…red band," he said.

Loussan handed the instrument over and Tolan injected himself beneath his chin. His skin solidified slowly.

"What is wrong with you?" the pirate asked.

"Faceless augmentation is a bit hit-and-miss," Tolan said. "The fleshshaper I hired wasn't quite as skilled as he let on. Bargain-basement prices, bargain-basement results…but it got the job done." He studied Loussan and tugged at his face until it matched the other man's. His hair went blond and stretched down to his shoulders.

"No, stop that right now," Loussan said.

"'Stop that right now,'" Tolan repeated in Loussan's voice.

Loussan slammed the case shut and made for the door.

"Fine, fine," Tolan said, his vocal cords wavering with different timbres. "Just had to get it back under control. Can't use a face the Daegon might know." Tolan's countenance shifted to an olive

188

complexion and a V-shaped face.

"Give me my shit back." Tolan held out a hand and Loussan slipped the handle over his fingers. "I didn't intend to become such a…connoisseur. There's a fair number of compounds I have to take to keep this up." He stood and his joints snapped as he grew several inches. His shoulders rounded and the muscle tone of his neck and arms improved. "Those compounds come with side effects. Painful ones. I don't know if you can consider them habit-forming, but if I go without for too long, my epidermis and epimysium will liquefy. So while I was tooling around wild space hunting Ja'war the Black…I had to find some way to maintain. And once you develop a drug addiction, the tendency is to push your collection as far as you can."

Tolan wiggled his jaw back and forth. The spy had a completely different appearance from when Loussan came in.

"Freshly fried flying fish, freshly fried flesh." Tolan's voice lowered an octave. "Strange strategic statistics…And so what if I like to expand my consciousness from time to time? You don't know me. Fuck off, you square."

"The Daegon will be here any second," Loussan said, gesturing to Tolan's open robe.

Tolan closed the flap. "I'll change."

****

The crew of the *Cassio* née *Joaquim* stood at the top of the cargo ramp. Tolan wore loose robes, his wrists heavy with gold bracelets. Earrings with jewels the size of a pinky nail and gold chain necklaces completed his outfit.

Geet stared at him, his jaw loose.

"What's the matter?" Tolan asked in his different voice. "This is how I choose to identify. Don't judge me."

"The good captain's underneath all that?" Geet asked.

"*I'm* your good captain," Loussan snapped.

"Everyone knows their cover story?" Dieter asked. "The station crew likely slagged their memory cores when the Daegon took over. That's the Concord thing to do."

"So the Daegon won't know who you are," Tolan said, "or any of us. Just let me do the talking and do not—" he wagged a finger at Loussan, "—let Jack out of his box."

"Who's Jack?" Geet asked.

Tolan gave him a gentle pat on the top of his head.

Warning lights spun up and the ramp lowered, revealing a ram's-head helmet of a Daegon officer in onyx-black armor and a vermillion cape. Close to seven feet tall and exuding malice, the officer ducked down and came up the ramp before it set down. One hand snapped and a serrated knife appeared. The Daegon didn't break his stride as he snatched Tolan off his feet with one hand and pinned him against the bulkhead, feet dangling.

The knife went against the side of Tolan's throat and the spy did his best to smile. "Welcome aboard." Tolan chuckled then winced as the blade nicked his flesh.

"I am Triarii Isaac. You are…" the Daegon grumbled.

Tolan could just barely make out the man's

eyes behind the lenses of the ram helmet, and he felt like he was face-to-face with a predator. His armor was badly scuffed and one shoulder was deformed, almost like it had nearly melted.

"Captain Zayif at your service," Tolan said. "The *Cassio* is at your disposal."

"Why are you here?" Isaac asked. "You arrived with no cargo."

Tolan kept his face even, knowing that a wrong micro expression might give away a lie. How the Daegon knew about their lack of cargo upset his belief that the invaders had lost any information from the station…he was either bluffing or he'd interrogated the longshoremen or customs agents. Tolan now had to worry about whether people could stay bought in Concord.

"Passenger charter," Tolan said. "People were paying seven hundred troy a head for transport into wild space. My broker promised a full hold…but ah…here we are."

Isaac lowered Tolan to the ground but kept his knife in place. "I don't know your kind," Isaac said.

"My tribe comes from Nuristan. Now part of Mechanix territory. I've been something of a wanderer for years. Do the Daegon know the adage about rolling stones and moss?"

Isaac tightened his grip on Tolan's robes and the knife drew a thin line of blood.

"It's useless and not worthy of your time, surely." Tolan glanced at Loussan, who had one hand over a pocket, ready to press a button within that would summon Ruprecht the Katar and make an enormous mess of the cargo hold in the process.

Scraping his thumb against his left middle finger, Tolan signaled to Loussan that he had things under control.

"Any of your crew of Albion?" Isaac asked.

"None," Tolan said as he winced and shied away from the blade.

"Come!" Isaac shouted over his shoulder.

Themata carried a partially opaque coffin up the ramp, a Daegon woman with silver foil over her face and upper chest inside. Two brutes with skull helmets flanked the coffin, one a head taller than the other, one arm hanging limp at one side, a carbine held across his chest with the other. The shorter man carried a shock maul.

Keoni poked the maul into Loussan's chest and asked a terse question.

"You will depart for Albion," Isaac said. "One of my soldiers requires specialist medical care not available on this piss bucket of a world. As I speak, the slip code is being added to your navi-computer…and my men are fixing a bomb to your hull. It will go off in eighty-six hours. You depart for Albion immediately and you will arrive in eighty-four hours…if this ship is as fast as you claim."

"Oh, she is," Tolan said. "We can make the run in—"

"Deliver my soldier to the planet's rulers and the bomb will deactivate. You'll receive new instructions afterwards. If she dies on the way, the Daegon will make you suffer, feral. Is this clear?"

"Crystal, Triarii, very crystal," Tolan said.

Isaac snapped the knife away, whirled around, and marched back down the ramp.

"You try and enter any other slip-space equation, you'll be destroyed," Isaac said as he exited the ship.

Tolan touched the shallow cut on his neck, noting a thin line of blood on his finger. He wiped his hand on Geet's sleeve.

"I say…" he said, waving up at Keoni standing outside the door to the captain's quarters, while the taller one removed his helmet and stuffed it under the crook of his limp arm, "does our VIP require anything before—"

Keoni smacked the head of his maul against a railing and sparks shot off.

"Master Henry," he said to Loussan, "skip everything and let's get going. Time is of the essence. See that our guests are comfortable."

"How comfortable?" Loussan rubbed a growing bruise on his chest.

"As much as they want," he said and flicked the "under control" sign at him again. As Tolan hurried off to the bridge, he did a double take at Seaver. The brute almost looked familiar.

As he passed, he listened to the other themata crouched against the bulkhead in exhaustion. They spoke with Albion accents.

Tolan fought back a smile as he went to the bridge and steered the *Joaquim* away from Bucky Station and back to home. The Daegon gave him a golden ticket to continue his mission, but his cargo, and the bomb on his hull, were new problems.

"One door slams shut and a ventilation shaft opens," he muttered.

****

Seaver let his mind wander as the down hours continued aboard the ship. With Juliae resting inside the captain's quarters, he hadn't left his post outside her door since they made slip space. The surviving themata slept against the lower cargo deck, occasionally crying out from nightmares as their minds processed the fighting on Concord.

His arm ached. His breathing had a slight catch from all the dust and God-knew-what-else he inhaled after the nuclear blast. And he kept seeing Powell's body every time he tried to relax.

"Some tea?"

Seaver snapped back and brought his carbine

up, his injured arm jerking uselessly. The ship's captain was there, holding a silver tray with several small clear glasses. How had he snuck up on him?

"Don't disturb her," Seaver said. "Go away. Now."

"It's for you," the captain said. "You haven't moved for hours. Haven't eaten. Drank anything. Tea?"

Seaver rolled his tongue around his mouth, tasting metal and blood. He took a glass and downed the tepid liquid with a swig.

"Albion's light burns," the captain said quietly.

"And I carry the torch," Seaver replied automatically, then he gripped his carbine tighter and glanced back at the door to the captain's quarters, afraid that Juliae had heard him.

"What have they been feeding you, James Seaver?" the captain asked.

"How do you know my name?" Seaver's brows furrowed and he set the glass back onto the tray.

"We've met." Tolan's face shifted to a lighter

tone and a different shape as he altered his voice. "Police action back on Albion just before this whole shit show started. 'James. Did you see anything? I didn't see you either. Let's keep it that way.' Remember?"

"That was you? But that means you're a faceless and...wait, that's illegal," Seaver said.

"Neither here nor there, bucko. I'm going to go out on a limb and trust you a bit. Got some news for you...your mother, ship's doctor aboard the *Orion,* she's alive," Tolan said.

"She is?" Seaver's bottom lip quivered for a moment. He sucked it back and bit it to stop.

"She is, and I'm working my way back to her and the *Orion*; just have a bit of business to conduct on Albion first. What say we ditch these Daegon assholes and go back together? That sound like something you'd like?" Tolan asked.

"Yes, absolutely, but there's..." Seaver motioned to the port on his collarbone and back at Juliae's quarters.

"Not right *now*, obviously," Tolan said. "We've got a slew of problems to deal with first. Help me help you, yeah? Tell me how you ended up as a bodyguard to an actual Daegon and what they've done to you."

Seaver recounted his capture on Albion, impressment into Daegon service, and his transformation into a shaped soldier.

"Translation device?" Tolan asked.

"An implant behind my jaw," Seaver said.

"That's useful. Hold still." Tolan removed one of his garish earrings and clipped it onto Seaver's earlobe. "Your Cro-Magnon look doesn't fit with my bling, but that's all right. Mars-derived tech…just like I suspected."

"What are you getting at?"

"Babelcubes," Tolan said, touching where his jaw met his ear. "Expensive bits of tech. I spent years tooling around wild space. No time to learn the language of every shithole planet I went to. Local Martian peddlers would update my cube for a nominal fee, made blending in a lot easier if you know the lingo…the software's close enough…my implant has newer code to it. Interesting."

"Why are the Martians using Daegon tech?"

Seaver asked.

"You've got it the other way around, kiddo." Tolan's eyelids quivered. "These Daegon are just as human as we are, skin color notwithstanding. Best I can piece together is that they left Earth sometime before the Great Eruption knocked the planet back to the Stone Age...now they're making their way back home."

"The Veil," Seaver said. "She said something about the Veil before."

"The band of nebulae and stellar phenomenon that block slip travel to the spinward side of the Centaurus Arm of the galaxy," Tolan said. "Maybe travel through there's not so impossible, yeah? Maybe I should go ask our VIP a few questions?"

"You can't." Seaver nudged an elbow at a Daegon device over the handle. "It's keyed to the legio. You fiddle with it and he'll know."

"Oh. Guess I'd better give up and resign myself to being a slave." Tolan gave Seaver a blank stare.

"You're going to—"

"Yes, I'm going to find a way in. Don't insult me…I need you to stay quiet and trust that I know what I'm doing here. I mean, I did get the Daegon to send me straight back to Albion with a golden ticket through customs," he said.

"How'd you manage that?"

"Dumb luck and patience, but imagine what I can do if I'm actually trying. And speaking of trust, you need to drink this tea in the next forty seconds." He rotated the tray and brought a glass closer to Seaver.

"Why?"

"Tick tock. Dead serious, by the way."

Seaver shrugged and swallowed tea more bitter than the first glass.

"That's the antidote to the poison I gave you earlier. Don't give me that look. If you were fully brainwashed and not on board with my agenda, I couldn't have you snitching on me, could I? That legio of yours doesn't seem too bright. You keel over now, he'd likely blame all the radiation you took when the Concordians decided to go out on their own terms. Fanatics, but you have to admire their resolve."

"They…fought harder than Albion did," Seaver said.

"No, kiddo, that's where you're wrong. We're not done fighting. Albion does not surrender. The Daegon have us on the back foot, but Commodore Gage has a plan, and the royal family is still with us."

"Prince Aidan? There were rumors…"

"Prince Aidan." Tolan nodded slowly. "Now, that legio of yours. He have any vices?"

"He's like any soldier that's survived too many battles. He lives for the now when he can. You have any cigarettes or alcohol aboard?"

"I'll scrounge around." Tolan removed the jewelry and snapped it back onto his ear.

"My mother…is she OK?" Seaver asked.

"Was the last time I saw her. Interesting lady, but she didn't care for me."

"No, she wouldn't," Seaver said. "What can I do to help, to get the hell away from these monsters?"

"Mum's the word for now, kiddo. Just act as normal." Tolan tapped his temple and left.

****

Keoni closed the door to the captain's quarters where Juliae lay on a slab covered by a semi-opaque shell on the bedframe, the mattress removed. She wore her armor from the waist down, her torso covered by a wrap of pearlescent cloth and her upper chest and half her face encrusted with a silver foil that lifted and closed like gills.

"Not such a sleeping beauty, are we?" Keoni pressed the hilt of his shock maul against a panel and the shell over the Daegon's head lowered into the slab. Keoni gagged as the smell of dead flesh and iodine wafted out.

Looking over a screen with Daegon script, Keoni's mouth moved as he read, then touched a key. The silver foil compacted against Juliae's skin and she gasped, eyes opening wide.

"No! Too much, too much!"

Keoni hit another key and Juliae relaxed.

"Legio…where am I?" she asked

"Aboard a feral vessel. Triarii Isaac sent you to Albion for care," Keoni said. "You're in bad shape."

"You sound…off," she said.

"Pidgin's tough to manage." Keoni popped the top off a small case and pressed a blue button against her throat. Her face quivered, then her eyes went soft. Keoni's visage drifted to Tolan's, though the hard angles of the legio's face were still there. "Now that I've got you on one hell of a sedative…we can have a chat while I work. I don't like using flurazepam, but I can't have you remembering any of this. Hand, please."

Tolan picked up Juliae's arm at the wrist and pressed his palm to hers.

"Father will be so proud," Juliae said. "I earned scars. I killed the ferals. Worlds brought back into the fold…under rightful rule."

"Just need to borrow some skin cells," Tolan said. "Give my blood marrow a sample so I can match yours. How invasive are your security screenings?"

"You can be my *vilicus*," she said. "Better that than to go home…nothing left for you."

"Where's home for you?" Tolan looked at his hand and his fingerprints morphed. "Is that where your father's at?" he asked using Keoni's voice.

"Palatine is no home," she said. "Caves. The poisoned sky. I'll have my stead hold on a world with rain I can drink. Just like Earth. Just like the Earth we left."

Tolan touched a port just behind her elbow.

"Genevans have these. I wonder…" He touched three fingertips to a small screen and a drawer popped out of the slate. Inside were pieces of her armor. He lifted up a V-shaped part that would cover her lower back.

"Genevan AI cores aren't in the head section, too obvious of a target. They keep them around their waist. I might need this later. Hope you don't mind." Tolan put the piece back then asked, "Can I go with you to Palatine, Centurion?"

Juliae laughed, then broke into a hacking cough. "There's no way back through the Veil," she said. "No way back…only victory."

"And how did you get through the Veil?" Tolan glanced at a clock on the wall and tucked her hand next to her side. His flesh went the same shade of purple and his face smoothed out to match hers.

"The Oculus. The Oculus is there. No way back, legio. No way…"

"And where is the Oculus?" Tolan leaned over her, his face twisting back to Keoni's.

"I don't know. Don't know."

"Of course you don't. You're a low-tier foot soldier with a high chance of being captured. Why would the Daegon let you know something that valuable? Figures…" Tolan plucked the injector out of her neck and pocketed it. "But you gave me a name, which is more than I had before."

He tapped her on the forehead. "Enjoy the hangover," he said before closing the shell back over her and leaving the room.

Seaver was still on guard just outside.

"Jesus, you look just like him," Seaver said.

"That's the point, kiddo," Tolan said. "Any issues?"

"One themata got up to take a leak. Everyone else is still asleep."

"Keoni's blackout drunk with the kicker I slipped in his drink, but if there's any questions…"

"He was here to check on the centurion. I

didn't hear or see anything else," Seaver said.

"Good. Nice and simple. Now, if you'll excuse me, I need to go slip into something more comfortable before everyone wakes up for breakfast. We'll arrive at Albion soon."

"And then?" Seaver asked.

"Then we improvise." Tolan winked at him.

****

As the *Joaquim* came out of slip space over Albion, Tolan leaned forward in his captain's seat, trying to take in everything over the planet at once.

"Daegon orbital control pinged us," Loussan said. "And we're being painted by targeting radar."

"Where is everything?" Tolan asked. "All the star forts are gone. Mistal Station…gone."

"The passive sensors on this tub are better than most Reich tech," Dieter said from a workstation just behind the two at the controls. "I'm pulling in data now."

"Nothing active." Tolan raised a finger. "Nothing says 'Please come and give this ship a white-glove inspection' like a radar pulse. Which is why I sprung for the top-of-the-line passive systems. Well, I didn't pay much. The Mechanix raider ship I came across didn't need them anymore."

"We're cleared for New Exeter spaceport," Loussan said. "We've got thirty-five minutes left on that bomb on our hull, for your information."

"Then execute the landing sequence chop-chop," Tolan said. "I know you're used to your neat little pirate chain of command, but if there's a ticking bomb involved, just do what you think is prudent before it goes off, yeah?"

"I have the conn," Loussan said with a sigh and the ship angled down toward Albion.

"The stealth drive?" Tolan asked Dieter.

"It passed all tests," the Reichsman said. "But the deeper we get into a gravity well, the more strain it'll put on the generator. It's meant to mask movement in and out of slip space and intra-system travel. Don't think I can flip a switch and make us invisible just outside…that. What the hell is that?"

Over New Exeter, a Daegon vessel nearly as wide as the city hovered overhead. The dome bristled with weapon emplacements, and landing bays built into the bottom hull were nearly as thick as the taller buildings on Albion.

"I saw that on my way out of here." Tolan swallowed hard. "Sends a message, doesn't it?"

"It's impossible," Dieter said. "It's larger than the *Bismarck* and it's just...there."

Sensor data scrolled across Tolan's screen and he swiped it toward a holo emitter at the front of the bridge controls. A diagram of the planet and surrounding space came up.

"I didn't know Albion had a void yard that big." Dieter pointed at an icon in the holo.

"We don't." Tolan touched the icon and it filled the space. A giant lattice filled with Daegon destroyer analogs in various stages of construction rotated slowly. Tolan moved the holo up and down an assembly line, watching as the ships grew from keel to final hull plate installation.

"Weeks to build one of those is my guess," Loussan said. "But where do they get the crews?"

"Where do you think?" Tolan asked. "Albion slave soldiers are back there." He motioned to the door. "Press gangs working aboard a ship isn't too much of a stretch, is it?"

"Risky," Loussan said. "Wild-space clans that relied too heavily on slaves ended up suffering an awful lot of 'accidents' when they got underway."

"But they're only building the escort ships," Tolan said. "Not their battleships or cruisers. And here," he said, swiping the holo over to Uffernau, Albion's ice moon. One of the ancient impact craters of the dead satellite was full of concentric rings, like a target. Cubes made up each ring, and robots swarmed through them like ants on a dead animal.

"Supply yard," Loussan said.

"Lots of supplies…more than enough for the number of ships the Daegon have in orbit," Tolan said.

"Sensors pick up a dozen battleships just on this side of the planet," Loussan said. "Who knows what's in the dead space."

"Plenty of logistics, not a whole lot in orbit…" Tolan tugged at his bottom lip, accidentally pulling it into a tag that jutted out from his mouth.

"To support the invasion, obviously,"

Loussan said.

Tolan tapped his lip back, saying, "Warships aren't logistics haulers. You see any cargo ships?"

"Not theirs." Loussan pointed ahead. A mass of void ships were anchored over the north pole, an eclectic mix of Albion-designed hulls, as well as Indus and Cathay and ones and twos of other star nations.

"Why destroy what you can use?" Tolan said. "Something seems off. Why not load those ships down now? The Daegon are on the offensive. Those supplies should be moving to the front."

"A staging area?" Dieter asked. "My father was no fighter, but he worked the yards during the last Reach War. The Reich built up the Potsdam System just before Francia launched their…war of aggression and were subsequently conquered in short order by our glorious Kaiser."

"Then what—or who—are they staging for?" Loussan asked. "The Daegon armada isn't here."

"Unless there's another one on the way," Tolan said and slumped back in his seat.

"How can there be more?" Loussan asked. "The Daegon already have more warships on the attack than…than the Reich and Indus have combined. And they might have *more?*"

"If they do, Gage will need to know," Tolan said. "The League will need to know. We've already gathered a fair bit of intel…"

"Then we should just leave now," Loussan said. "I'll have Mr. Ruprecht take care of our passengers and—"

"Can he disarm the Daegon bomb on our hull?" Tolan asked. "We're setting down in the capital. Leave the rest to me. Now, if you'll give me a moment…I have an itch I need to scratch."

"Now? You're going to get high now?" Loussan asked.

"Shut up and fly, monkey." Tolan pushed out of the bridge, bumping into the bulkhead on rubbery legs.

Chapter 15

Gage walked onto the bridge and to the command holo tank where Price was waiting for him.

"Your shadow's lagging." She raised her chin toward Thorvald's customary spot.

"Reassigned for the duration of this mission," Gage said. "I'm not taking any chances with Aidan's safety."

"Fair enough. Ten minutes until we exit slip space. All ships are at battle stations and fighters at alert condition one for immediate void operations," Price said.

"I'm all for dealing with this situation without a fight, but better to be ready for one than not." Gage opened a fleet-wide command channel and the other captains appeared in the holo. Birbal and Han were together, the Cathay officer looking sour.

"Eleventh, the pleasure is mine," Gage said. "Plan remains unchanged. We will exit slip space around the dwarf planet Taisan and attempt to make contact with the 5th Fleet. My intention is to bring them back into the fold and exit the system without engaging the Daegon if possible."

"And if they're unwilling?" asked Captain McGowan of the *Sterling*.

"Then I will declare them traitors to the Crown and we will deal with them as a hostile force," Gage said. "You all know Albion's history. Never has a captain abandoned the kingdom. Never has one of us ever surrendered while they still have the means to resist. We will get to the bottom of what's happened to the 5th Fleet and why they turned on the Cathay."

"Admiral Nix, she graduated within a few years of you at the Academy, correct?" Captain Erskine of the *Valiant* spoke up.

"Correct," Gage said. "She was two years ahead of me, but I knew her from the fencing team and we served together aboard the *Starfire* for a time."

"Helpful, one would hope," Erskine said. "We can determine if that really was Nix in charge when they hit the Cathay…and if it is her, she'll know you."

"This…I want all of you to understand that the worst-case scenario is possible. We may have to fire on our own ships," Gage said. "Dealing with a rogue element is not what I want to be doing right now. I'd rather be coordinating with the League for an operation to liberate Albion…but if we do not bring this matter to a close, there will be no League beside us. You know what happened to Francia when there was no one to save them from the Reich. We cannot let the flame go out. Is there any among you that cannot fight against our own if—God forbid—it comes to that?"

"The Albion Navy is no fair-weather organization," McGowan said. "We swore to protect and defend King and country. Everyone in the 5th did the same."

"No issues," Erskine said.

"None," said Captain Vult of the *Ajax*.

Each commander joined in the sentiment.

"The *Arjan Singh* is at your command," Birbal said. "Do forgive us for any Albion lives we may take…should it be necessary."

"We'll be far harder on ourselves than on you, Captain," Gage said. "General Han, you said there's a small mining outpost on Taisan, correct?"

"Yes." Han's mouth worked from side to side. "The outpost may not be known to the Daegon as…the facility's paperwork wasn't exactly in order."

Gage raised an eyebrow. An illegal operation in Cathay space wasn't implausible, particularly if the right people were paid off to keep the goods hidden from the Emperor's tax collectors.

"That may be to our advantage." Gage looked up at Price through the holo, then to Clarke on the bridge. The XO called Clarke over.

"Let's make ready," Gage said. "Albion's light burns."

The captains saluted and Gage returned the courtesy.

"XO, ready comms jammers and have the master-at-arms prepare an away team," Gage said.

"Aye aye." Price put one hand to her ear and

spoke into a mic on her wrist.

"Ready slip emergence," Lieutenant Vashon announced.

The *Orion* lurched back into real space and the dwarf planet Taisan popped into the holo tank along with the rest of Gage's fleet. The planetoid was small and covered in ice. Not too dissimilar to Pluto or Eris, Gage thought.

"Confirm we came in on the dark side of target planet," Price said. "Our arrival should be masked to the Daegon deeper in system…unless they've got sensors out here. Comm jamming in effect."

In the holo, a small settlement and a cleared landing pad appeared at the base of an ice mountain as the ship's sensors swept over the surface.

General Han appeared in the holo. "Gage…let me hail the settlement," he said.

"Not possible at the moment," Gage said. "A wide-spectrum pulse might be detected by the Daegon."

"I know their dish code. I can connect with a tight-beam laser. No way the invaders can pick that up from out here," Han said.

Gage and Han stared at each other for a moment. That the Cathay officer knew the illicit facility's hailing frequency and its capabilities meant that Han was neck-deep in corruption. But did Shin know about this too?

"I'll allow it," Gage said, then sent a message to Birbal and waited.

"Nothing else on our scopes, sire," Price said. "Orders?"

"Get us in closer to Taisan, make it harder for us to be detected," Gage said. "Ready passive probes for a slow orbit. We need to see where everything else is in this system."

A new window opened in the holo and a Cathay man with disheveled hair and dirty mining coveralls appeared.

"To the great and powerful Daegon forces," the man began, "we humbly surrender and apologize for not announcing ourselves to you—"

"Shut up, Chow," Han said. "Wait, the Daegon don't know about you?"

"Han? But we thought—"

Han spoke in a Cathay dialect that the *Orion*'s translators failed to recognize. The back-and-forth between the two men bordered on shouting.

"The Daegon haven't been here…yet," Han said. "Though this dog has been laying out the welcome mat for them."

"If they haven't been out here, why is he…" Gage trailed off as data from the mining facility hit the holo tank and the view changed from the close orbit of Taisan to the entire Basai system.

"We—I mean the undocumented miners— have sensor platforms across the planet," Han said. "Helps them know when inner-system security ships are on the way out for their regular inspections."

"And that's when the facility goes into hiding," Gage said. "The landing pad retracts beneath the surface and the air locks get covered up by sensor dampening material that look surprisingly like the methane ice chunks that are all over the planet. Right?"

Han shrugged.

"Wait, these Albion aren't with the invaders?" Chow asked.

"We are Albion," Gage said.

In the holo, a small group of red triangle graphics appeared between the orbit of a gas giant and Taisan. Gage touched the new plots and the holo zoomed in on Albion ships on course to the dwarf planet.

"We saw them coming," Chow said. "My crew and I debated on hiding, but we thought there wouldn't be anyone coming to help us. We don't have a ship, or even enough food or water to—"

"How many personnel do you have?" Gage asked.

"One hundred and twenty-five."

"Get them to the air locks. I'm sending an away team to move you to the Indus ship *Arjan Singh*," Gage said.

"That's very kind of you," Chow said, "but there is a matter of ore. This planet is rich with deuterium isolates, and if we—"

"Shuttles will be there in thirty minutes," Gage said. "Pack light."

"Clarke," Gage said loudly, "patch in to the sensors and ready a Klieg message."

"A what?" Birbal and Han appeared in the same frame.

"Old Albion navy trick," Gage said. "Our sensor arrays have a certain bandwidth that's reserved for telemetry data and routine ship traffic. Certain less scrupulous sailors will use it to send off-the-record transmissions."

"You're going to contact the other Albion ships now?" Birbal asked. "Why not wait until they come around and—"

"Because I have faith," Gage said. "Look here." Gage swiped a hand across the holo to Basai where a Daegon fleet of nearly a hundred vessels loitered over the wrecked dome city. "The Daegon are too far away to catch us if we need to retreat back into slip space. We need time to generate a slip equation that will get every Albion ship out of here in one go. If I wait until the 2nd Fleet arrives, the Daegon could attack us."

"What's wrong with fighting Daegon?" Han asked.

"Beating them here doesn't help anything," Gage said. "This system is lost. The city…gone. I need ships and I need Albion sailors to liberate our home. Losing lives now helps nothing."

"To hell with the Cathay, right?" Han asked.

"I'm getting your people out, aren't I? And I'll be sure to leave out a number of key details when I speak to Shin," Gage said.

Han pressed his lips together and looked away.

"Why send every Albion ship out here?" Price asked.

"You heard the miner. Deuterium isolates," Gage said. "Expensive material. Used in slip-engine construction. The Daegon must want it."

"They're letting the 2nd Fleet off the leash," Price said. "Slip equations are easy to generate farther out in the system…"

"The Daegon must think the 2nd won't run off if it has the chance," Gage said. "That's…that's something."

"Shall we abort?" Birbal asked.

"No. No, let me contact Admiral Nix first," Gage said, pulling up projected times for the 2nd Fleet's arrival at Taisan and how long it would take the Daegon fleet to make the same journey from the inner planet.

"We've a couple hours on our side," Gage said as a green box popped onto his control panel. He touched it and a text message field opened.

"Come on, Nix," he said under his breath, "be the person I know."

He began typing.

****

Gage paced in his wardroom, glanced at a timer, and grumbled.

Emma came into the room with a tea tray. "Sire...care for a spot?" she asked. "Still have plenty of Twinings...but if you get me in a Cathay market, there are a few of their blends I think you'd enjoy." She set the tray on a conference table and clasped her hands over her waist.

"Thank you." Gage took a sip, glanced at the sugar jar, then drank more.

"Bertram taught me how you like it," she said.

"How's he doing?" Gage asked.

"Bertram? He was a bit rattled with what happened on New Madras—a chilly dunk like that and then coming face-to-face with that Daegon hunter…he's so brave!" Emma flushed slightly.

"I promoted him," Gage said. "He's doing well with Prince Aidan?"

"The Prince insists on having Bertram in the room when he falls asleep," Emma said, lowering her voice slightly. "I think Salis is jealous."

"I'm sure she can cope." Gage took another sip.

A message alert came up on the table.

"Sir, it's the *Heracles*," Price said from a speaker in the ceiling.

"Very good," Gage said, setting the teacup down. "Go."

Emma took the tray away.

Gage adjusted his uniform and pressed his thumb to a reader on the desk. A holo panel appeared at eye level, the window filled with static. Gage ran a hand down his face, wondering how long it had been since he'd slept.

"Thomas?" a woman asked.

In the holo was Admiral Nix. She was a few years older than him, the beginning of crow's feet at her eyes and blond hair run through with a few strands of gray.

"Michelle," Gage said and managed a smile.

"I'm in my quarters," she said. "I got your Klieg…couldn't believe it when it came up in my messages. I knew the 11th was out at Siam. Then we got the news from New Madras about Aidan and…"

"The Daegon let the word out that they were beaten?" Gage asked.

"Beaten? They killed Aidan. We saw—"

"Prince Aidan is alive," Gage said. "He's with me on the *Orion*."

"He…is?"

"Albion lives, Michelle. We still carry the torch," Gage said. "What happened to the 2nd?"

"He's alive…" Nix put a hand over her mouth for a moment, then composed herself. "We were anchored over Sandov when the Daegon attacked. We had no warning. One minute everything was normal and then…then the comm channels were full of 'novis regiray' and they were right on top of us.

Admiral Harelson tried to organize a fight, but then one of the Daegon infiltrators killed him and…command fell to me. You need to understand, Gage, there was no way out. The slip buoys were gone. The Daegon outnumbered us five-to-one and they were inside our shield wall. All I could think about were all the families we had down on Sandov station and…"

"You surrendered," Gage said.

"I did," Nix said, tossing her hands up. "I betrayed everything I swore to defend. But the Daegon aren't the Reich. They're merciless to a degree that—"

"I know." Gage held a hand up. "Believe me, I know how bad they are."

"That I was common-born kept me alive," she said. "They went through our rolls and arrested every officer with a noble title and…they spaced them. Made me watch them do it. A few days later, they ordered us out of dock and into Bardas' fleet and we were on the front lines of their advance through Kong space."

Gage gave her a quick rundown of his fleet's

actions since they slipped away from the Daegon at Siam.

"You're a better commander than I am," she said. "I always knew you'd go far, Gage. Though this isn't how I thought it would happen for you."

"I had a good teacher back in school," Gage said. "Now let's get focused on how we win this fight."

"Winning? I doubt that's possible," she said. "The Daegon occupy Albion, Thomas. They have Sandov. The Daegon have my sailors' families. My family. If we don't follow their orders, we're not the only ones that suffer. They…my gunnery officer tried to kill a Daegon. They brought his wife and children from Sandov to the ship and they…"

"Monsters," Gage said. "All of them. We have to throw them off Albion before they destroy everything we are."

"How? How do you think that can happen, Gage? I've seen their fleets. Seen firsthand how they steamroll worlds. There's no stopping them," she said.

"They're human. They can be beaten. I've

done it," Gage said. "And once the League finally responds, then the Reich and even Columbia will—"

"You think some grand coalition's going to turn the Daegon back?" she huffed. "We can't even get a formal treaty to end the last Reach War."

"This is different. The Daegon won't be stopped unless every nation in free space unites against them. Then we can free our home," he said.

"With Aidan alive, maybe the League will listen to you…Regent? Guess I should call you 'sire.'"

"Don't," Gage said. "I can get your ships out of here with me, Nix. Is there anything I need to know? Bombs they may have planted? More infiltrators in your crew?"

"You'll take us back to Kong space?" she asked.

Gage nodded slowly.

"You know what we've done to them." Her face hardened.

"You are my responsibility, not theirs," Gage said. "I won't just turn you—or any of your people—over to them."

"They have our families, Gage," Nix said. "If

we run off with you, they're the ones that will suffer."

The door to the wardroom opened and Salis came in with Aidan.

"Come here, my Prince." Gage lifted the boy up and held him at his side so Nix could see him in the camera.

"Sire," Nix said and bowed slightly, "I…I am honored to see you."

"Commodore Gage says we need you," Aidan said. "I want us all to go home together. To Albion."

"I want that too, my Prince," she said. "There's just…"

"What?" Aidan asked.

"Complications, sire. I don't want to frighten you with the details," Nix said.

Gage set the boy down.

"You and the 5th Fleet cannot stay with the Daegon," Gage said. "They will feed you into the grinder until there's nothing left of your command, and then there's no guarantee the others will be safe. Fight back. Come with me and we will never surrender. Never stop fighting until everyone is free."

"It's not that simple," Nix said.

"It is. Albion's light burns. We are the torch that lights the darkness, and we will never surrender. You know this, Michelle. You taught it to me at the academy."

"Simple words and phrases to fill midshipmen's ears is one thing," Nix said. "This is something far worse."

"You remember when the *Starfire* intercepted that smuggler outside Grant VII?"

"The slaver," she said.

"You and I opened the pens. I'll never forget that smell of all those people...you remember the children we rescued?"

"Of course I do," she said. "I adopted two of them."

"We are still Albion. We have our duties. Our honor. Our mission."

"You don't have to convince me, Thomas, but I can't speak for my entire fleet...not when families are on the line," she said.

"I'm sorry, aren't you still *Admiral* Nix?"

"I didn't exactly take a consensus when I gave in to the Daegon," she said. "There are a number of issues aboard my ship and others that I need to deal with. A few of us have gone completely over to the enemy. Not everyone has your resolve, I'm afraid."

"Just have your ships ready to jump out when you reach the mining outpost," Gage said. "We can handle the rest when we're back on Lantau."

"Give me time," she said. "I'll send you another Klieg when we're ready. It's good to see you again, Gage. Circumstances being what they are."

"Same here." Gage cut the channel and put one hand on the table.

"More of our ships?" Aidan asked.

Gage nodded.

"You're concerned," Salis said, taking Aidan by the hand.

"Something's off," Gage said. "Nix only adopted one child from the slaver ship we intercepted. Not two."

"Could she have been replaced by a Daegon?" Salis asked.

"Her Klieg code checks out." Gage tapped the table. "I included a challenge to her in my original message. An old Portsmouth Academy-ism that the midshipmen whispered to each other when the nobles were giving us trouble. I put 'lowborn sound off' in the message I sent. She responded with 'stronger blood.'"

"I don't get it," Aidan said.

"It was a silly thing young and immature midshipmen said to each other, a sentiment we learned was ignorant and foolish after we got into the fleet. I'm ashamed of it now, my Prince, but it was a code I used to make sure Admiral Nix was truly Admiral Nix," Gage said.

"Then the error with the adopted children?" Salis asked.

"I don't know yet…but we need to be ready for anything," Gage said.

"Aren't they our friends?" Aidan asked.

"They are, my Prince," Gage said, but he didn't believe the words. Not completely.

****

Nix stood with her head bowed in her quarters. A man and a woman in dark clothing were on either side of the doorway; both had deep-green skin and dark hair.

"Interesting," the man said.

"The boy…should be dead," said the woman.

"Prince Aidan isn't relevant," Nix said. "Please, Inquisitors, I'm sure there's a way to please Lord Bardas without putting more risk on his—"

"Silence." The woman raised a finger and the torque beneath Nix's high collar tightened ever so slightly.

"What say you, Megeth? Why let the thralls know their Prince is dead when he still lives?" the man asked.

"The rumors about Baroness Asaria and Tiberian must be true," the female inquisitor said. "She's either covering for his failure or he lied to her, Lucian. Either way…"

"Albion must never know the boy still lives," Lucian said. "Hope is a poison. Daegon thralls must learn to love the lash, isn't that right, Nix?"

"By your will, masters," Nix said.

"This one understands," Megeth said. "But what of the rest of the thralls on this fleet? They may turn on us."

"The boy must die," Lucian said. "And Lord Bardas must know of this."

"If you send a message back to Bardas, Gage will know and he will bolt," Nix said. "He's just like the Kongs when we first arrived in this system. He'll welcome me with open arms. One quick strike and…perhaps the rest of his fleet will give in."

Megeth chuckled. "Be serious, thrall. This Gage of yours doesn't have the same grip on reality that you do. His fleet is tainted by defiance. They never bared their throats to us as you and yours did," she said.

"What if our thralls learn the boy lives?" Lucian asked.

"They submitted to your rule when they knew he'd escaped Albion," Nix said. "Nothing changes."

"They'll destroy the *Orion*?" Lucian asked.

"They will," Nix said and raised her chin slightly. "We know the price of disobedience."

"Lord Bardas will want to bring in his ships," Megeth said. "Overwhelming force wins battles quickly and with minimal losses to us. The Albion thralls have proven most valuable to us…it would be a shame to lose too many in a fair fight with Gage's ships."

"We have the element of surprise with us," Nix said. "A dagger in the night is worth more than a thousand swords at dawn, yes?"

"Bardas is aggressive," Lucian said. "If we even hint at Gage and Aidan being within reach, he will strike."

"But he appreciates a slaughter," Megeth said. "We strike the feral Albion first, then bring Bardas into the fight. He will forgive our oversight of not alerting him beforehand, so long as he can go to Asaria with a scalp."

"Yes…yes, this will play out well for us," Lucian said. "Your performance is commendable, Nix. We will bring any surviving Albion into your command."

"Thank you, masters," Nix said and bowed deeply.

Chapter 16

Themata carried Juliae down the ramp to a drone cargo shuttle bobbing up and down on four anti-grav engines. Seaver pushed the slab onto the drone's bed and clamped it down.

A Daegon in simple fatigues with a fist sigil on his chest touched a slate and the drone rose up toward the *Sphinx* hanging over the city. He spoke to Keoni and the legio led Seaver and the themata away.

Loussan ran a hand through his long hair, feeling the sharp humidity of New Exeter's weather. Dieter and Geet stood behind him, their shoulders hunched like hand-shy dogs.

The Daegon came up the ramp and sniffed at the sailors. Green highlights on his cheekbones and forehead over his purple skin gave him a different look than most of his kind.

"You're restricted to your vessel," the Daegon said. "Await reassignment. You step foot on this planet and you'll be arrested."

"Thank you, my lord," Loussan said, bowing deeply. "There is a matter of refueling and the bomb—"

The Daegon tapped his slate and there was a crash as the bomb detached, sending a shock through the *Joaquim*'s crew.

"You're last in priority for fuel. You wait. This your entire complement?" he asked.

"We've suffered a recent tragedy," Loussan said. "Our captain made a medical error and…expired." He motioned to a black body bag on the deck behind him. "He was of a strange faith. He must be buried in black soil with his head pointing back to Earth at the time of the last shovelful of—"

"Incinerator," the Daegon said, snapping his fingers. A pair of longshoremen ran up the ramp and carried the body bag away.

"Incinerator?" Loussan put a hand to his

mouth. "But, sir, he was a godly man. At least let him—"

The Daegon backhanded Loussan and sent him crashing into Dieter.

"Anything else?" The Daegon raised an eyebrow, then turned and left, holding his slate behind his back.

"What do we do now?" Dieter asked Loussan as he helped him back up.

"What can we do?" the pirate asked. "We need fuel. We follow the plan until we have other options."

"Plan?" Geet asked. "What plan?"

"Go clean something; that's your part of the plan," Loussan said.

"Yes, Captain." Geet nodded quickly and hurried back into the ship.

"I hate Albion and all her jackboots." Loussan hit a button on the cargo bay frame and the ramp pulled up. "It's still got jackboots in charge, just ones worse than the last."

****

Seaver and the remains of his themata—what had once been almost a hundred soldiers and was now eight men—followed Keoni into the star port's customs area. He remembered the building from a childhood trip off world to visit his mother on shore leave to some unsettled world full of saurian wildlife.

All trace of Albion authority was gone; flags and portraits of the royal family had been ripped away and not replaced. Keoni took them past empty inspection stations and into the administration area in the back where four Daegon soldiers waited for them. One yanked Seaver's carbine away and pinned him to the wall with one arm, while the other soldiers disarmed the themata quickly and without finesse.

"This standard," Keoni said, putting one hand to his head, fighting a hangover. "Your world. No trust."

A Daegon put a palm on Seaver's armor and the plates fell off. His mail bodysuit went slack and he felt its weight. The soldier grabbed him by his injured arm and forced him into a cell meant for those that ran afoul of Albion customs and immigration. The door slammed behind him and locked with a magnetic hum.

The rest of the themata went into neighboring cells, but Seaver was the only one locked up alone.

"Legio...did we do something wrong?" Seaver asked.

"Masters won't make you fight on your home world, but you no free here. Themata your home. Not here," Keoni said. "You stay here until Juliae is up. If she no...then Daegon give us new centurion."

"I can't see my family?" a themata asked. "Can I tell them I'm OK? Are they even still alive?"

"Stay," the legio said and turned away, ignoring pleas from the other themata.

Seaver slunk down on the cell bench. Looking out a small barred window, he saw the *Sphinx* high above.

Maybe Tolan could get him out of here...maybe this was just another day in the last few months of his life. His wounded arm ached, and a tremor grew in both hands. His heartbeat pounded in his ears and he touched the small vial attached to the port on his collarbone. The pale-white liquid inside was down to the last few drops.

He was linked to Juliae, and if she died, he knew he wouldn't outlive her by much. Even if Tolan did get him off world…maybe he could see his mother one last time.

Seaver lay down, but sleep never came.

Chapter 17

A garbage truck came to a stop outside the spaceport. A black bag fell off one side and rolled into a trash-strewn alley until it pressed against more bags of refuse piled high around an overloaded dumpster.

Tolan's hand shot out of a corner and he ripped his way out, panting and covered in sweat.

A cat hissed at him and bounded away.

"Hello to you too," he said as he ducked around the dumpster and took out a small metal mirror. Looking himself over, he put a slight bend in the bridge of his nose. This was a blue-collar area, and a few battle scars were expected.

He stood up and stretched, breathing in the

smell of old garbage, and held his arms to the *Sphinx* overhead.

"Not good to be home," he said, dropping his arms. "Not good under these circumstances." He removed a cigarette from a case, pressed the filter against his neck, and got a quick hit from the compound that kept his skin and muscles in order. Then he flipped the cigarette around and lit it. The drug had many names across Wild Space, that recreational druggies appreciated the substance managed to keep demand—and supply—up wherever he went. He preferred to call it Bliss.

"Let's see what we've got." He walked out onto the sidewalk and looked at a holo sign over a corner. "Right shitty neighborhood. Just missed my stop by a block."

A drone with a camera dome on the bottom passed overhead, and he turned away and started walking toward a watering hole with a faded sign. The Anti-Grav. It was almost dusk, and he didn't hear anything from inside as he approached, which made the hair on the back of his neck stand up in worry. The door was open, though, and it got him out of the drone's line of sight.

Down the middle of the space inside was a long bar lined with stools, while mostly empty booths and a few tables filled up the floor. Holo monitors were all switched off.

As he came up to the bar, Tolan kicked a broken glass aside and scanned the nearly empty bottles in rows against a long mirror. The bottle he was looking for was missing, and he wasn't sure what that meant.

A man came out of the back and stopped near him on the other side of the sticky bar. He had a metal torque around his neck, and his skin was raw around it.

"You must have got off shift early," he said.

"Accident, too dangerous to keep us around while they cleaned it up," Tolan said. "You got any Chivas Noble?"

The bartender paused. "If I did, how you take it?"

"Olives and a sprig of yeast extract," Tolan said.

"By the King, I thought they got everyone in

the resistance." The barman leaned close. "Where's your torque? You have one, the Daegon will kill you if they think they have a reason. No torque—they'll kill you for fun."

"I've been in the Eastern ranges with a partisan team," Tolan said. Hinting that he'd come from off world recently would narrow the Daegon's efforts if this barman wasn't on the up and up. "Came in from the cold for some decent news. How's the ministry holding up in the city? Ormond?"

"Ormond's still active." The barman's eyes snapped to a couple in a booth across the bar. "These Daegon…they've got the city in their grip. Every operation we tried ended with dead agents. Any that were captured…I keep the holos off because all the Daegon broadcast are executions at sunrise and sunset. Rest of the time, the cameras are on bodies hanging from the city walls."

"Jesus," Tolan said, touching a tumbler with the side of his hand. His field craft demanded he get a drink to look like he'd come into the bar for its intended purpose, but he wouldn't have minded a quick drink either.

"You have script?" the barman asked.

"No script out in the boonies," Tolan said.

"There's nothing coming in." The barman picked out a bottle of whiskey and flipped it over to pour out a shot. "Stock's running low. They'll probably grab me in the next impressment sweep. I've got a knee replacement that kept me low on their desirability index, but if the Daegon need warm bodies for something…they get warm bodies."

"What've we gleaned about them?" Tolan asked. "There's got to be more than their name and that the Reich are Boy Scouts compared to them."

"They just want us to obey, not to understand." The barman sighed. "Any noble they find? Executed. Any blood relation to the royal family? Executed. Direct rule. Our resistance plan was drawn up against the Reich and Cathay…we weren't ready for this."

"Albion's light still burns," Tolan said. "We'll never be slaves so long as we keep fighting."

"That's the thing," the barman sneered. "The Daegon have a word. *Sippenhaft* or *sippenhaftung*. You attack a Daegon and they come after your family—

246

not just your immediate relatives either; generations removed. My cousin got the neck for someone in Devon that cursed out one of the beast's foot soldiers. Never even knew the guy that got him killed. I lucked out."

The door to the bar opened and three men walked in, each wearing coats too heavy for the summer weather. Tolan watched them using the mirror behind the bar and set his drink down as the new arrivals made straight for him.

"Lucky, eh?" Tolan raised an eyebrow. He reached into his shirt and gripped the snub-nosed pistol taped to his flank. He fired three times, the muzzle blast blowing out the back of his shirt and burning his skin.

The lead man pitched back, taking two hits to the chest while the third round grazed his face and exited out a window in the door. The second man tossed the corpse aside and lunged at Tolan with a blackjack in hand.

Tolan ripped the pistol free and hit the man's striking arm with the butt of his gun, earning a sharp cry of pain. Jerking the weapon back, Tolan shot him in the face.

The third man threw a chair at the spy's face and clipped his head. Tolan fell hard on his side and rolled back as the attacker stomped down where his head had been. Tolan fired by accident and blew the man's foot off at the ankle. He went down screaming, clutching at his bleeding stump.

The spy rolled one last time and thrust his pistol at the barman as he made it to the back door. His vision swimming, he shot the traitor in the back and he slammed into the door. It swung open, dropping him with a meaty thump.

Tolan swept his gun back to the couple in the booth. The woman had her head tucked against the man, who had his hands up and out to ward him off. The man pushed his date behind him to protect her, and Tolan brought his aim to the man bleeding out on the bar floor.

"You're a cop," Tolan said. "I've seen you before."

"I'm sorry," he said, his words slurring as shock set in. "They...no choice. Get me some help? I'm getting cold."

Tolan shot him in the heart and hurried out the back door, grabbing the barman by the collar and dragging him into an alleyway. He knelt next to the body and produced a knife hidden in his belt. The flex blade went rigid with a snap of his wrist and Tolan sawed through the torque in seconds. He put it around his own neck and gave the barman a pat on the shoulder.

Tolan's face changed to fair skin, and a thin beard grew as his cheeks puffed out; the spy seemed to gain twenty pounds as his body morphed.

"They don't even let us have guns," Tolan said as he pulled a line out from his watch and wrapped it around his pistol grip, then tossed the weapon down the alley. It caught fire and melted within seconds. "Which means me carrying one just won't do. You got any of that script for me?"

Reaching into the barman's back pocket, he pulled out a fat wallet. He stripped off a covering on his jacket, changing its color and style, and stripped off a similar layer on his trousers. He tossed the crumbling wraps into a dumpster and ran off as the sound of sirens grew.

The resistance—if any was left—was compromised. He needed to find Ormond, the director of the Intelligence Ministry, and finding that man would be nigh impossible…even if he was still alive.

"I should've stayed on the ship," Tolan muttered.

****

Inquisitor Syphax stepped over a puddle of blood, the providing corpse still lying in it. He was short for a Daegon, but well built. His sea-green skin stuck out like a neon sign against black hair, its onyx sheen catching in the light of the bar. Stooping next to a fallen stool, he swept a palm over it, tiny filaments in his skin glowing.

Daegon soldiers stood silently along the walls as the inquisitor picked through the aftermath of Tolan's shootout.

The couple that witnessed the event huddled together in their booth, a Daegon lording over them.

"Please, sir," the man said, "we've told you

everything we—"

Syphax lifted a finger and the man's pleas stopped. The inquisitor went to the bar and ran a fingertip along the rim of a spilled glass, then raised a phantom gun to the doorway where the barman had been shot, then back to the three dead Albion quislings.

"Explain yourself," Tiberian said, striding into the room. He kicked the leg of the nearest corpse and sniffed hard at the smell of blood and waste released by the bodies soon after they expired. "Why did you call me here?"

"Welcome, Lord Tiberian," Syphax said, "we've a situation here. One that either concerns you or will interest you."

"Slaves killing other slaves is beneath us," Tiberian said. "Have the legio organize a purge as a lesson to the others and be done with this."

"I don't expect you to instantly grasp what happened here," Syphax said. "The barman was of the Albion Intelligence Ministry. Somewhat removed from their operations, but kept on as a fixer and operative in the event the planet fell to invaders. We coopted him early on and used him as bait for any ministry agents that our initial sweep failed to remove."

"You're boring me." Tiberian crossed his arms over his chest.

"And this bait caught a fish," Syphax said. "Proper challenge and response to tell the barman that he was part of the ministry. Our agent did as required—he called in the local constabulary to make an arrest…and things went off plan. One feral operative in the wind is of some concern, but then it gets interesting."

"Does it?" Tiberian studied the bullet wounds in the dead quislings.

"Our surveillance cameras picked up this individual entering the bar." Syphax tapped the side of his fingers against the back of one hand and flicked toward the broken mirror behind the bar. A projector built into the racks holding glasses cast Tolan's image onto the mirror. "Matches the description the witnesses gave," Syphax said. "Matches the face we caught in the back alley."

A grainy video of Tolan tossing his clothes

away and taking the barman's wallet played on a loop next to the screen cap of his face.

"But then we got this." Syphax tapped a fingertip to his bottom lip and a new video of a taller man with long hair, but wearing Tolan's same clothes with the same bullet-exit damage on his shirt appeared. "And this."

A video from a traffic camera displayed the same man, now in a filthy shirt, running away from a topless indigent and into a crowd. A screen capture from a shopping center showed an olive-skinned man wearing the same shirt.

Tiberian put his hands on the bar and small talons unsheathed from the gloves and bit into the wood.

"Yes…now you understand," Syphax said. "Tell me, Lord Tiberian, what happened to the Faceless you dragged out from the prison beneath the palace? You presented him-her-it to Baroness Asaria…and then?"

"He went by Ja'war," Tiberian said. "I got him aboard the *Orion* with orders to bring me the boy…I assumed he was dead."

"Why?" Syphax asked curtly.

"Because I chased down Prince Aidan on New Madras and saw him die," Tiberian said. "The Faceless failed in his task. I sent a wide-spectrum code to activate the kill switch we implanted in his chest during our…withdrawal from the planet. If he was still alive anywhere in the system, the kill switch would have ended him."

"And yet…" Syphax paused to gesture to the different men projected on the broken mirror, "and yet there is a Faceless loose on Albion. One could craft a working theory that the blank of a man you pulled out of the prison cells was an Albion agent, one that tricked you with a promise to find Prince Aidan, and one that found his way back here aboard your fleet."

"Don't blame me because you've lost control of the security situation," Tiberian said. "This Faceless technology the ferals devised isn't uncommon."

"That's where you're mistaken, my lord," Syphax said. "The Faceless are in direct violation of the Vitruvian Accords that every 'civilized' system was a party to. Such bio modification like this is an instant life sentence on Albion and a capital offense in many other worlds. The Faceless are denizens of wild space, not here."

"Your hypothesis depends on me being a fool," Tiberian snarled, "yet leaves no room for a second one of these freaks to exist."

"I accept that there may be another," Syphax said, "which is part of the reason I called you here. That there is a Faceless in play is not up to debate, yes? But your responsibility for this occurrence is in question."

"Ja'war the Black is dead," Tiberian said. "A failed tool. I finished the hunt for the last of the royal family." He brushed his fingers over his new writ. "Do a mass DNA sweep of the city. You'll find this new one easy enough."

"Faceless can mimic DNA of anyone they've come into contact with," Syphax said. "Sweeps are pointless. The glass this one used has nineteen different DNA prints on it and this establishment had a reputation for cleanliness. There's a predator on the loose, my lord. One that needs to be hunted down."

"You admit you're incapable of handling this, do you?"

"Your reputation as a hunter precedes you, Tiberian," Syphax said. "Part of my writ is to secure Baroness Asaria from any threats stemming from the conquered population. This Faceless is a challenge to my talents and capabilities. To bring in expert assistance like yours seems prudent and reasonable, yes?"

"You imply that I may be at fault so I can join the hunt," Tiberian said. "Any damage caused by this Faceless from here on out can be blamed on me. That's your game, Inquisitor."

"My writ is my own," said Syphax as one side of his mouth pulled into a smile. "But now that you've hunted down a small child...I thought you'd appreciate a true challenge."

Tiberian ripped part of the bar off and swung it at Syphax's face. The splintered end just missed the inquisitor and Tiberian let the hunk fly into the glass behind the bar, shattering it into fragments.

Syphax held his ground, a smirk on his face.

"You bring me here and you insult me,"

Tiberian said. "You imply I'm at fault for your mess, then dangle a challenge. Which is your true purpose, Inquisitor?"

"Are you on the hunt or aren't you?" Syphax asked.

"I will find this Faceless of yours," Tiberian said. "Not because I share any responsibility for your failings, but because I have nothing else to amuse me while I wait for my fleet to be repaired."

Syphax rubbed his palms together. "Excellent. Let us cast a wide net and—"

"No," Tiberian snapped. "We move and we betray ourselves. Our prey blundered into this trap; he'll be cautious from here on out. I have a better plan. Guards," Tiberian said, glancing at the two witnesses, "execute them. They've heard too much."

Tiberian and Syphax left through the back door, the snap of two gunshots following them out.

Chapter 18

A fishing trawler pulled into the docks of New Exeter's harbor, and men hauled boxes of ice and squid onto the back of a small truck. They worked silently, tired after so long on the water. A Daegon drone drifted by, but the crew gave it no attention. Such security measures were the norm, and anyone on the occupier's bad side knew they wouldn't last long in the open.

A fisherman on the far side of middle age went to the captain and collected a small stack of script. He tugged at the torque around his neck and made his way out of the docks, ignoring the stink of dead mollusks clinging to his body and going right past the seedy bars that catered to far fewer workers than had frequented the area before the invasion.

Going up a hill to his tenement, his eyes darted over the windows and paused over a single horizontal slash across the corner of a pane of glass. He put a hand to the knob and stopped, fingers trembling, then squeezed the handle. The biometric sensor unlocked the door with the clack of two bolts.

He opened the door slowly and the night's breeze wafted past him into the dark room.

"'Assume you're being watched at all times and you'll never fumble,'" Tolan said from inside.

The fisherman shut the door behind him and shrugged off his coat.

"If you're compromised, say so now, Ormond." Tolan emerged from the shadows, gun in hand. His face was narrow, and lanky brown hair clung to his head.

"I'm clean." The head of the Albion Intelligence Ministry closed his blinds and turned on a holo set with a wave of his hand. He nudged the volume up and sat heavily at a small round table. "That you, Tolan? It's hard to be sure."

"It's me." Tolan leaned against the kitchen

sink and rested his pistol against his thigh. "How'd you guess?"

"I don't recognize you, but you know the field craft to send the right signals." Ormond jerked a thumb to the window with the mark. "Though…I don't remember you being authorized to see the backup identities for senior ministry staff in case of occupation."

"I got bored and decided to have a little peek around the office before the Daegon showed up," Tolan said. "Our internal security measures needed a massive overhaul. I was going to tell you, but…" He raised a palm up. "You had a reputation for fly-fishing. I figured you might take this backup persona."

"Big difference between waders and a rod and hauling inkies out of the bay," Ormond said, squeezing arthritic hands. "Were you there…when it happened?"

"Bring me up to speed," Tolan said.

"The Daegon claim that Prince Aidan is dead." Ormond's eyes spoke to repressed tears. "I trusted him with you, Tolan. What happened?"

"Last time I saw the Prince, he was just fine aboard the *Orion* with Commodore Gage. Had to finish off Ja'war the Black before I bid them farewell."

"Huh…knew I should've put that dog down before we abandoned the palace," Ormond said. "You weren't at New Madras?"

"No, I got to have all the fun at Concord. Look, there's lots of second-guessing to go around, lots of loose ends. Gage sent me back to Albion to make contact with the resistance and gather intel for his plan to liberate us. I'm assuming he has a brilliant plan and sent me here to help that all come together. So here I am. This is winning. I suppose."

"There is no resistance," Ormond said, shaking his head. "The Daegon didn't come here to rule by proxy. They didn't just install a new governor and leave a garrison to collect taxes." He pointed to the ceiling and the *Sphinx* high above. "They erased every institution we had. Every government building was demolished but the palace. Every civil servant, military veteran, and anyone with a bit of clout or social standing were swept up and sent to the themata regiments or to the shipyards as labor. We never…never in all those years of planning, accounted for an enemy so thorough. So ruthless. We've gone from a kingdom to a planet full of slaves in a matter of weeks."

"Bullshit." Tolan levelled a finger at him. "There's still fighting in the provinces. The Daegon can't control every single—"

"They're chasing around the last of our military for sport," Ormond said, raising his chin to the holo. In the projection, a half-dozen emaciated men and women in tattered Albion uniforms walked up a gallows where nooses were put around their necks.

Tolan squinted at the hangman—a Corps commander that had fought during the Reach War.

"They don't kill just you," Ormond said. "They kill your family. Your neighbors. People you work with. They don't *need* us for our skills, Tolan. We're laborers…cattle—and no, they don't need talented cattle."

"I don't believe it," Tolan said. "Our light burns. We are the torch against the darkness. How can—"

"They hanged King Randolph and Queen Calista over Remembrance Boulevard," Ormond said. "They made everyone in the city walk beneath the bodies. Anyone that refused, they killed. Anyone unable to show up because of illness or injury, they killed…unless they had a healthy relative that could be dragooned into the Daegon's service. Think of that, Tolan. My entire adult life in service of the King and Albion, and I…I obeyed the Daegon."

"You're an intelligence professional," Tolan said. "Let's not pretend that personal integrity or external appearances mean anything to us. You appeared to bend the knee, now you're off the enemy's radar. Well done."

Ormond wiped a hand across his mouth and leaned back in his seat, staring at Tolan. "Why did you mention Commodore Gage? I sent you to Admiral Sartorius—"

"Dead. Killed by a Daegon deep operative before I could even link up with the *Orion*."

"Does…Gage know?"

"Know what?" Tolan asked.

Ormond sniffed hard and put his elbows on the table. "I slagged the air-gapped systems just before the palace fell and I ran off into the boonies," Ormond said. "Kept the Daegon from knowing our backup personas and assets we had hidden around the planet to fight an occupier…they still managed to capture and torture enough of us that the plan fell apart. But Gage…you think he's still alive? The Daegon claim they won at New Madras."

"He's no slouch in the commander's chair," Tolan said. "Smart. Clever. Listens to reason. For a common-born to reach his rank, he can't be mediocre at his job. But if the Indus fell there…"

"There's a nature-or-nurture argument we might have if we live that long," Ormond said. "Where's Gage now, you think?"

"Maybe best we keep some details unsaid," Tolan said, glancing around the room. "The Daegon…what have you learned about them? Where do they come from?"

"I laid low in a data relay center just outside the city when they first took over. Looked through slip-space logs from just before their arrival and…it doesn't make any sense. Their fleet came in from three different systems—at slip points we thought the math impossible to solve for—but there they were. They came in from Sevastopol, Moku'Ume and star Epsilon Tau-Exi."

"A pirate mining world," Tolan mused, "some nowhere settled by Polynesians and…"

"A star in the Veil," Ormond said. "Impossible, isn't it? There are no slip-space lanes through the Veil. No hard-bore routes. You move there at sub-light speed, and even that's difficult with all the nebulae and dead star systems."

"You heard of anything called the 'Oculus' before?" Tolan asked.

"Some of my sources working the logistics yards have heard the Daegon mention it. Where'd you learn that word?"

"Daegon mentioned it," Tolan said. "We can reject what we think is impossible, or we can acknowledge that there's a floating city full of purple and green cunts overhead—and not long ago, I would've said that was impossible. And that's it? All you've gleaned is from stellar cartography?"

"Their language is mostly ancient Latin," Ormond said. "The Daegon names tend to be European and tied to old rulers. Their skin…no idea why they're like that. No one on Earth was blue or green back then."

"They don't take to radiation well," Tolan said. "I…never mind."

"Don't trust me?"

"Trust is one thing. Torture is another. Doesn't matter what they do to you—God forbid—if you're burned. But you can never give up information you don't know," Tolan said. "How can there be no resistance? You hear about Concord?"

"The Daegon announced they conquered it."

"That bunch of hillbillies nuked themselves rather than surrender to the Daegon," Tolan said. "When this is all over with, you want the history books to hold them up as heroes and mark Albion as a bunch of bootlickers and cowards?"

"Harsh, Tolan. The way things are going now, there'll only be the official Daegon account of what happened here."

"No." Tolan shook his head. "Gage will bring

the League into the fight. I just need…I need to go back to Gage with more than your sad sack of a story. He's a military man, not a politician, so if I can just…" He looked to the holo and sighed slowly.

"You have a way off planet?" Ormond asked.

"Yes, I'm going to morph myself into a being of light and transcend space and time to reach Gage," Tolan deadpanned.

"Yeah, yeah, what I don't know…" Ormond rolled his eyes. "The people, the average man and woman out on the street, they had hope. They had hope until they told us Aidan was dead."

"The Daegon show the body?" Tolan asked.

Ormond shook his head.

"Well then…I'm not one to take their word about anything. Where does Albion's light shine the brightest?" Tolan tapped his chest just above his heart.

Ormond looked away, ashamed.

"Curfew's in another twenty minutes," Tolan said, picking up a small satchel. "I helped myself to your wardrobe. Thanks."

"Wait, take this back to Gage." Ormond went

to a cupboard, pried open a wooden slat, and tossed a glossy black chit to Tolan. "It's gene-locked to senior officers. Contains King Randolph's…orders to any surviving commanders. I kept it when I slagged the ministry's files."

"This at all relevant," Tolan asked as he slipped the chit into a pocket, "given how every other plan we've had went straight to shit?"

"Do it, Tolan. I know you don't care for much in this galaxy, but get that chit back to Gage. It's vital to the war and to keep Albion's light burning."

"Spoken like a true believer," Tolan said. "Don't contact anyone else. Word gets around that I'm here, it'll only make my job harder."

"You know where to find me." Ormond took a nearly empty bottle of clear liquor from the freezer and unscrewed the cap. "Even though you're a freak and clearly unstable…it's good to see you again. Gives me hope."

"Always a pleasure." Tolan gave him a mock salute and slipped out the back.

Ormond took a deep swig from the bottle and

watched the front door.

An hour later, he was a sip away from finishing when Tiberian smashed through and seized him by the throat.

****

Hunched over and walking with a cane, his face that of an elderly woman's, Tolan watched as a Daegon shuttle lifted up from the street outside Ormond's home and flew off to the *Sphinx*. Tolan shuffled down a sidewalk, mumbling to himself.

Three Daegon, a pair of soldiers and a youngish-looking man in combat fatigues, exited one of the row houses.

"You," said the young one, thrusting a knife hand at Tolan. "You're in violation of curfew." He unsnapped a pistol holster.

"Oh, I'm most dreadfully sorry," Tolan croaked. "I was at Mary Elizabeth's for bridge and the bus decided not to show up. I've had to walk for miles and my corns…oh, my corns are just awful."

The Daegon drew his pistol.

"My son serves aboard your them-atas."
Tolan pointed to the sky. "Commands a whole
squadron in your noble service. Please…I'm all he
has. Help an old woman up the stairs and he'll be
such a good servant to all you lovely green people. If
he learns I was put down so close to home…"

*"The Baroness has ordered leniency for those that
serve,"* the young one said in Daegon to the soldiers. *"I
will take the crone home and see her son whipped as
punishment."*

Tolan's translation device was working just
fine, he was relieved to realize. He worked his jaw
back and forth to disable the auto speak systems.

"His name?" The Daegon went up the short
staircase and pushed open the door for Tolan, who
took his time getting up.

"Mike Jones," Tolan said.

The Daegon tapped at a tablet and shook his
head. "I'm a compliance officer and there are
hundreds with that name," he said. "His thrall
number? It's on his torque." The Daegon tapped his
neck.

"Oh dear…I have it written down inside. My

memory isn't what it used to be. I tell you, that Mary Elizabeth uses that to cheat at bridge. I had a four-jack trick and she kept going on and on how that's not the game we're playing and I told Mary Elizabeth I know the game *she's* really playing and she wasn't going to get my ration book if she kept cheating."

Tolan shuffled past the Daegon, who snarled at him then glanced at the two soldiers before following the "elderly woman" inside.

The Daegon emerged a few minutes later, his attention on his slate.

"Get the slave's ID?" a soldier asked.

"I did. No point in having him whipped; he was killed when we pacified Concord. She didn't take the news well." He put a hand to his chest and tilted his head to one side, earning chuckles from the soldiers. "Saves us the trouble of putting her down with the next culling."

"Send for a cleanup crew?" a soldier asked.

"No." Tolan tapped his slate. "Some inquisitor has the area on high alert. No services. Let the slaves pick up the smell in a few days. They'll take care of the mess for us."

"Finish our sweep?" a soldier asked.

"No, back to the garrison," Tolan said. "The inquisitor's recalled us. Perhaps we need to process another batch of thralls for the shipyard."

"How long until we can send every last one of these ferals to the incinerators?" a guard asked. "They're barely worth the effort to keep as slaves."

"What's the point of ruling an empty planet?" the other guard asked. "Every Daegon will have at least a hundred slaves on the reconquered worlds. Just as was promised by the High Houses."

Tolan followed the guards as they led him back to the garrison, adding little to their conversation. Looking up at the *Sphinx*, he prayed Ormond would forgive him.

Chapter 19

Tiberian stood outside a circular room. Ormond was hanging by his heels, his naked body dangling over a bloodstained grate. Pulsing cables ran from Ormond's temples and the base of his skull to a device on the floor. Although the screams didn't bother Tiberian, the interminable period he'd spent waiting for Syphax to get results did try his patience.

Syphax stepped away from Ormond and tossed a bloody pair of pliers onto a tray. The inquisitor removed a pair of goggles from his head and tapped them against his thigh, knocking away flecks of blood.

"You want me to show you the right way?" Tiberian asked.

"Eighty-two percent of the subject's nervous system registers pain," Syphax said. "Any more and he'll go into cardiac arrest. Any less and I'm not taking my craft seriously."

"He's given you nothing," Tiberian said.

"The norm for the senior Albion intelligence caste. They believe if they can hold out for two days, everyone they're in contact with will have time to go to ground. I've seen this before," Syphax said.

"You're just going to have him attached to the Excoriator until then?" Tiberian asked, his anger growing. "You're on thin ice with me, Inquisitor."

"But we've found ways around that belief system," Syphax said. "Watch and learn."

Syphax went to Ormond, who was convulsing with pain, drops of blood shaking loose and pattering against the floor. The inquisitor swiped a finger across the Excoriator and the lines attached to Ormond's head went dim.

"Hear me?" Syphax asked as Ormond's body slackened. "I found your DNA in the palace. In the King's antechamber. In a number of high offices. You were important. No fishmonger."

"Albion's…" Ormond spat out a glob of blood, his lips flapping against toothless gums. All his teeth had been yanked out soon after his arrest, a precaution against suicide devices. "Her light…"

"I know," Syphax said, patting Ormond on the back. "I've heard it all from much stronger men than you. I know how long you think you need to hold out, but let's skip all that, yes? Who came to visit with you? How can we find him?"

One side of Ormond's face twitched, and Syphax didn't know if he was trying to smile or if his nervous system was on the verge of a convulsion.

"One of our slaves identified you as a senior operative in the intelligence ministry," Syphax said. "Imagine our surprise when your public file had you as a simple laborer. Albion may have destroyed some of its more sensitive records, but DNA doesn't lie…does it? In fact, with enough samples, we can track down most anyone's relatives across the planet."

Syphax raised a hand and a door slid open. A Daegon soldier walked in, leading three children by chains.

Ormond's breathing picked up, almost

hyperventilating.

The children broke out crying, screaming for their grandfather.

"You see…Director Ormond," Syphax said, "children can't keep secrets. But they can feel pain."

"No…" Ormond struggled against his bonds, dangling like a fish about to die on a line. "No, please don't hurt them."

"Little ones like that can grow to be useful," Syphax said. "If I attach them to this same machine, they'll be ruined. And the Daegon don't bother with damaged goods. Now…who came to see you?"

"Little Stephanie…don't let her see me like this," Ormond said.

"Tiberian!" Syphax called out. "Choose one."

"He's…he's Faceless!" Ormond cried. "Could be anyone. Name…name is Tolan. He was a poor agent. We sent him—sent him to wild space almost as a joke. He wasn't supposed to come back at all. But he did. He did…"

"There, that's progress," Syphax said. "Now keep answering my questions or I'll have Tiberian peel the skin from your favorite granddaughter in front of you and her sisters. Tell me everything about Tolan."

****

Tolan remembered Falkland Square as being a bit more avant garde compared to the rest of New Exeter. Cheaper rent in the surrounding hab blocks attracted artists and students from the nearby university, and the park and fountains at the south side of the square had a reputation for hosting events that the city's more proper citizens would have never attended.

He walked along the edge of a pool where the new and functional fountainheads beneath the water were switched off.

Tolan—in the guise of an elderly man with a cane—thought back to years before, when he and his team of intelligence ministry agents had decided to go for a meal at an authentic Thai restaurant near the square just before their mission to wild space.

The names and faces blurred in his memory, but long-dormant feelings of happiness and comradery came to him as he retraced his steps from that day. The Intelligence Ministry had been his passion. He believed every word of the mantra that Albion's light burns, and the small kingdom was a beacon of hope and justice on the edge of anarchy where pirates and despots ruled on the fringe of settled space.

He looked around to shuttered shops and restaurants. Battle damage from the invasion still lingered, with low piles of broken bricks and walls leftover from the Daegon attack simply pushed to one side of the road instead of removed completely. Smoke and soot stained a building, leaving a dark outline of where a ground car had burned next to it.

New Exeter felt like it had just been murdered, its still-warm body in full view of horrified passersby.

"What now, eh?" he asked. "What's left to save…"

"You!" Two men approached from behind, both wearing armbands with the double headed eagle Daegon crest and carrying nightsticks. "These are assigned work hours. Why aren't you at your job?"

"Not much I can do," Tolan said, mincing forward with his cane. "The Daegon gave me this." He swiped a liver-spotted hand across the torque on his neck. "Told me my dear grandson Johnny was in a them-atta or something and I'd be allowed to live. They took Agnes and Elsie and even Beauregard away. Beauregard lost his legs fighting the damn Reich." He spat and almost hit one of the men's shoes. "Fine man. Fine man he was! You two are spry-looking…why didn't the Daegon take you?"

"They do what they want," one of the men said and tapped his own torque. "Can't say no."

"Well," the other said, "we could, but that would be the last thing we ever did. Get back home, old-timer. Go before one of their damned inquisitors sees you. There's no mercy from them. No chance for an explanation. You step out of line and you die right then and there or you disappear and are never seen again."

"Sound like right assholes," Tolan said, then ducked slightly and whispered, "Don't tell them I said that."

"This way." One of the men pointed down a

street and helped Tolan along. "And don't tell them you said what?"

"I didn't hear anything," the other said, shrugging.

"See, there's hope for us all yet." Tolan quickened his pace slightly. "These inky ones. You know their names? There's a pigeon that keeps eating all the sunflower seeds I've planted. I want to give that bastard a name so I can curse him out properly."

"One we've dealt with is called Syphax," one of them said.

"Now there's an asshole name if I've ever heard one," Tolan said. "More. Tell me more about him. I can't walk that fast and we've a bit of time."

****

Tolan, disguised as a Daegon compliance officer, made his way through what once housed the Albion Customs and Immigration headquarters. Their personnel were largely Daegon, but there were still plenty of Albion citizens working in the offices and walking the hallways.

Tolan walked with high confidence—head high, steps long. Albion personnel shrank away from him and pressed their backs to the wall as he passed, many of the female clerks hugging tablets to their chests as a shield.

The spy kept his mouth shut and readjusted four tablets he carried at his side. Nothing conveyed "I'm on my way to something important, leave me alone" better than someone loaded down with work, in his experience.

For appearances' sake, Tolan glanced up at a sign over a vault door. He knew where the servers were located, but a recently arrived occupier might not. He pressed his palm to a reader and his skin itched as it sampled the print and a bit of his skin and blood.

The door unlocked with a snap and he pushed it open. The DNA he'd sampled from the compliance officer he'd killed near Ormond's home had a decently high level of access. Trying to swap identities with a more senior individual was tempting, but the muscles quivering beneath his face hinted that would be a risk he couldn't take.

Inside, servers hummed and an air conditioner blasted cold air. Tolan let his guise slip a little and leaned a shoulder against a wall. Fishing out a pack of cigarettes from inside his shirt, he jabbed the butt against his neck.

"The hell?" He looked at the filtered end, slipped the smoke between other fingers, and pulled out another one. This one was loaded with the drug he needed, and he let out a little sigh as a tiny needle snapped from a hidden injector and poked into his jugular. His vision swam and his legs went rubbery, but he stayed on his feet. He put both cigarettes into his mouth and was about to light them when he shook his head and tucked them back into the carton.

"These bastards even smoke?" he wondered out loud as he looked up at a blinking fire alarm.

His face tightened back into the disguise and he tapped the corner of a tablet against a reader on one of the servers. A system access UI came up in Albian and Tolan's fingers hesitated over the screen.

"Here goes nothing." Tolan entered a code to a backdoor program and a sprite undulated on the screen. It expanded into a red and silver edge around the UI, telling him he'd gained access.

"Daegon take out the leadership, leave the worker bees alone to do all the work," Tolan said. "Why waste time retraining everyone? Logistics is logistics. Move this stuff to that place by such and such time and…my, my, what's this?"

Tolan swiped down shipping orders, his attention fixated on a particularly large file. He opened it with a double tap and his face drooped as he lost focus on his appearance.

In fifty-one days, a convoy would arrive over Albion. Tenders, fleet supply ships, and fuel ships carrying fusion cores were to be on standby and ready to service the new arrivals. What stuck out at Tolan was the number of ships on the manifest: over eighteen thousand. Each had a designation string that made no sense to Tolan, but he suspected it was a Daegon ship.

"Son of a bitch, how can they have that many…where are they coming from?" He read through the file but couldn't find the answer, so he went back to the beginning of the order and found that all the support ships were to anchor far above the northern pole. "That's the slip-space point they're coming in from…who wants to bet it's from Epsilon Tau-Exi out in the Veil? That many more ships added to the Daegon armada…no one will stand a chance."

Tolan looked out a window to a nearby building, the roof cluttered with antennae and satellite dishes.

"Hello, Void Control…hello, nav-buoy data," Tolan said. "Now, if I was Gage, what would I need to know…yeah, he'd want that. Don't want to come back to this well if I don't have to. Time for some hard decisions."

Tolan pulled down a menu on his slate and entered a code. While the slate downloaded data from the server, he tabbed through fields before finding what he wanted. A chirp rose from the slate and went on until a box popped open and a bleary-eyed Loussan answered from the *Joaquim*'s bridge.

"Captain Zayif of the *Cassio*, how may I be of service?"

"Drop the act, Loussan. It's me," Tolan said with a Daegon's voice. He rolled his eyes and squeezed the side of his Adam's apple.

"Say again? You're not sending a picture," Loussan said.

"It's me, your favorite jackboot," Tolan said with the voice Loussan knew. "How's my *Joaquim*?"

"Well, if the Daegon know all that, doubt they'd go through the trouble of taunting me with a call." Loussan sat in the captain's seat. "Ready for pickup? You got us an escape route?"

"I am…working on that, yeah." Tolan grimaced. "I've got a plan. One you're not going to like, but it's the best I can think up on short notice. Seems the Daegon have a significant emotional event planned for every free planet in settled space, and we need to get back to Gage ASAP."

"That wasn't our deal, you clay-faced ass. You promised—"

"My ship once I return to Gage with what he sent me here to get. You'll still get it…we just need some data first—particularly, slip codes to a star in the Veil and where Gage and the Free Albion Forces…are. Where they are. Yes."

Loussan tossed his hands up to shoulder level. "I should've surrendered to the Indus," the pirate said. "They don't even have a death penalty."

"But I know where both are, probably," Tolan said. "And that's where I need you to make a small sacrifice."

Loussan's jaw dropped slightly as Tolan laid out his plan.

"That's insane. And suicide," Loussan said.

"It's revenge," Tolan said. "Revenge for the loss of your ship, the *Carlin*, and all your Harlequin brother and sister crew that died when the Daegon destroyed her. That something you want?"

"It is," Loussan said, crossing his arms, "and it solves another problem for me."

Tolan tapped one temple, even though Loussan couldn't see the gesture.

"I'll send the supply requests. Assuming the system is just as efficient as the last time I did this, we'll be out of here in hours," Tolan said.

"Last time you did this?" Loussan asked.

"Being perfectly honest here," Tolan said, switching his voice back to the Daegon's, "the Intelligence Ministry has done some shady stuff in the past. One of my first assignments was to move some contraband through our own customs systems to launder it for delivery to a certain rebel faction. You're a smuggler. What's the easiest system to beat if you have to move product?"

"Lazy humans," Loussan said.

"Lazy humans…and confused humans, both are leverage points for me. Get everything ready. I'll signal you with a pickup location. Have the stealth drive humming," Tolan said.

"You'll owe me for this," Loussan said.

"You can't collect from my corpse, just so you know. The materials you need are in the scan-shielded compartments beneath the engine heat sumps. Don't act like you and Geet haven't found them already. Tolan out."

He set up another tablet and began tapping away with both hands.

Chapter 20

Syphax nudged Ormond's bloody corpse and the rope around the ankles creaked. The inquisitor removed thin blue gloves and tossed them into a small bin near the door to the cell.

"Subject expired, time stamp now," Syphax dictated and the words scrolled across a holo screen floating nearby. "Cardiac arrest due to system shock. Resuscitation methods ineffective. Shame; this one kept up some of the fight."

Syphax walked over to a rack and slipped on his overcoat. A layer of mail folded around his body and linked into the padded pants and metal-shod boots. The armor he wore doubled as his clothing, much more comfortable and elastic than the heavier suits Tiberian and his brutes preferred.

"System, summon Tiberian," said the inquisitor before going to a wall and waving a palm in an arc. A screen projected over the flecks of blood on the white paint, and he picked through data streams for a few minutes until Tiberian shoved the cell door open with a bang.

"Have something at last?" Tiberian asked. "I'm not your muscle or your parlor trick to intimidate prisoners."

"And here I thought you liked frightening children," Syphax said without looking at the other Daegon. "Seems to be your calling."

"You put that feral down already?" Tiberian jabbed a finger at Ormond.

"Heart gave out. It happens," Syphax said as he shrugged, "but he was useful."

"He tell you how to find the Faceless?"

"Not directly, but he told me enough. Tolan is a master of disguise and infiltration. He may even be able to pass as one of us," the inquisitor said.

"Heresy," Tiberian said, stroking his purple face.

"And where is the only place one of us would face difficulty getting into or out of?"

"The *Sphinx*," Tiberian said. "The Baroness allows only those of her inner circle aboard. Too many key facilities. The golem forge, our slip-drive engine foundry, most of our—"

"But once you're aboard…you're aboard. And anything we lose to sabotage there will not be replaced quickly or easily…or at all." Syphax pressed his knuckles to his chin as streams of data scrolled past and more windows popped open on the screen.

"There's only one way in or out of the *Sphinx*," Tiberian said. "The jade hangar where—"

"Look," said Syphax, stabbing at a report field as it scrolled across the screen and expanded to fill the wall. "A delivery of Albion ice wine from the star port to the *Sphinx*. The case is in transit now from the processing facility at the port…"

"How big is this case?" Tiberian asked.

"Not so dense, are you?" Syphax smirked. "Dimensions are large enough for a man to fit inside if he chooses to be uncomfortable. This authorization code…it's old. Albian. Where else has it been used?"

"Stop wasting time." Tiberian went for the door. "Stop the delivery to the *Sphinx* and let's go open it ourselves. Maybe we've caught the Faceless."

"What's this 'we' business? I've rerouted the shipment in question to a storage warehouse...and I'll have it packed in with other goods. Let's see him get out of there before we arrive."

"I'm not waiting for you," Tiberian said and left.

Syphax muttered a curse and pulled the data feed to his forearm, where a smaller screen appeared. He cross-referenced the Albian authorization code and frowned. It was used to order several more crates from the spaceport to different locations throughout the city. Strangely enough, the point of origin had been erased from the records.

"No matter," Syphax said, jogging to catch up with Tiberian. "We'll interrogate every worker until we find out where they all came from."

"What are you getting at?" Tiberian asked.

"Just being more thorough than you care to——
"

An explosion rattled the windows as distant

echoes of more blasts sounded through the city.

"When I catch Tolan," Tiberian said, breaking into a run, "I will rip his face clean off and make him truly face-less."

****

"What the hell was that?" Void Master Calixta asked as the lights in the orbital control center flickered on and off. The Daegon head of all movement in and around Albion's space lanes went to a workstation where one of the local technicians shrank away as she approached.

"This city suffer from earthquakes?" she asked the tech.

"No, master," the man said, "I…believe it was a bomb. The only time I've felt something like that was when you…when you arrived," he stammered, bending his head like a whipped dog.

Across the control center, Daegon and Albion staff spoke to each other as their screens cut in and out.

"Silence!" Calixta ran a finger along the edge

of her ear and opened a secure channel to the *Sphinx*. "Inform the Baroness that the city—"

Fire extinguishers popped from the ceiling and white foam streamed out, covering the floor, expanding up to waist height of the staff, and filling the control center with a thick mist. The Albion crew went into a near panic and were quickly shouted down by threats from the Daegon.

"Control, lock down all movement to and from the orbitals," a Daegon said through her earbud.

"Affirmative." Calixta wiped foam off a screen and keyed in her override. The screen flashed red with an error message: USER LOGGED INTO STATION 7B

"What?" The Daegon waded through the fire-retardant foam and scowled at the ceiling. The control center was Albian, and just why they designed the system to inundate the facility and all the equipment further cemented her low opinion of the ferals.

A tech bumped against Calixta in the foam and she swatted the woman aside as she made her way to a workstation in the back of the room. Glare from flashing screens filled the foam like lightning during a nighttime storm.

Calixta made out a lone figure working frantically as she lunged at the station, grabbing the tech by the shoulders and spinning him around.

Her own face stared back at her.

"Well," Tolan said with a feminine lilt, "this is awkward."

A pistol cracked twice and Calixta slumped to the ground, her heart and spine shot through.

Daegon shouted and rushed toward the commotion, but found Calixta's body with both hands clasped over her chest. Something in her grip began chirping, the sounds coming faster and faster. The bomb had just enough explosive force to wreck the control center and trigger the evacuation of the entire building.

Tolan slipped out with the crowd. Columns of smoke grew from several points in the city as he moved with the mass of Albion workers.

"Loussan, it's go time," he said into a communicator hidden in the palm of his hand. "You've got authorization from orbital command to unmoor, yeah?"

"Got it a few minutes ago," Loussan said through a bud in Tolan's ear. *"The entire grid just went haywire…something about terrorist attacks. Was that you?"*

"Labels, labels," Tolan said, rolling his eyes. "What's a freebooter like you to use them?"

"This pickup location…you know if our IFF doesn't check out, then—"

"I'm well aware. Just be there on time." Tolan's voice cracked and the pigment of his skin rippled through the color spectrum.

An Albion woman near him gasped as the crowd meandered toward a park.

"Don't breathe," Tolan said, putting a finger to his lips. "It's contagious."

The woman slapped a hand over her mouth and scurried away as Tolan ducked down an alleyway to a sack of clothes hidden beneath a dumpster.

****

Syphax drew a pistol as the doors to a warehouse opened. Daegon soldiers rushed past him and formed a perimeter around cargo containers in the middle of the space. Tiberian lingered in the doorway as the inquisitor made his way inside.

"How do you know it's not another bomb?" Tiberian asked.

"Drones scanned the air for the same explosive used at the other blast sites. Came up negative." Syphax signaled the soldiers and they began tossing crates and boxes aside. "But the box in question did have a higher CO_2 trace."

Drawing a sword from a belt and securing the scabbard to his waist, Tiberian said, "The Faceless destroyed power relays and communication nodes across the city with his bombs, and now you're convinced he's in there…with the intention of sneaking onto the *Sphinx*."

"Oh, I'm sure he's in there," Syphax said. "It will be most interesting to vivisect one such as him. They are rather difficult to catch…perhaps these ferals have a bit of technology we can use to improve our wraith infiltrators."

"He's shown talent thus far." Tiberian readied his sword and drew a pistol as the soldiers dragged out a coffin-sized cargo container. "To get caught like this…strikes me as sloppy."

"Overconfidence is the final mistake of many intelligence professionals," Syphax said. "Now…I need him alive." Putting a half mask over his mouth and nose, he removed a small vial from his belt, clicked the top twice and set it down on the container. A lime-green gas hissed out and wafted over the container.

"Enough nerve-paralysis toxin to take down an elephant," Syphax said, removing his mask as the gas faded away. "Let's see if he's got a look of surprise on that malleable face of his."

The inquisitor stomped down on the lock securing the lid and flung the top open.

A matte-black blade the width of a hand shot up and pierced Syphax through the heart. A click-click-click of a snake rattle sounded and Ruprecht, the Katar cyborg killer, sprang up. A mechanical arm hugged Syphax close and the blade erupted from the inquisitor's back. The Katar's soulless blank visor turned to Tiberian over the dead inquisitor's shoulder.

"Harlequins always balance the scales." Ruprecht's artificial voice warbled over the rattle from his body. He flung the impaled sword arm to one side and dropped Syphax inside the crate.

"Kill it! Kill it!" Tiberian backpedaled and opened fire with his pistol.

Another sword snapped from Ruprecht's other arm and he dove to one side so fast, he was a blur to Tiberian. The Katar rolled forward and thrust a blade out, cutting a Daegon soldier from his hip to shoulder.

Bullets sparked against the Katar's back and shoulders as he caught the dead soldier and tossed him up. A double cut from his sword bisected the Daegon at the waist and a kick sent the man's legs crashing into a pair of soldiers, knocking them down. Ruprecht poked the tip of his swords into the torso of the dead man and whipped around, flinging the remains into another soldier and snapping his neck so badly, only the armor on his neck kept his head attached.

Tiberian aimed carefully and shot Ruprecht in the center of his visor. Spider-web cracks spread across the glossy black glass and Ruprecht emitted a high-pitched squeal. The Katar spun at the waist, his torso rotating like a top on a spine servo, and tore through a group of rushing soldiers like they'd wandered into a thresher.

Daegon crowded around Tiberian to protect him as Ruprecht stopped. The Katar's arms swung forward and blades speared out and impaled a guard on Tiberian's left. The other blade pierced through the man on his right and embedded in the Daegon behind him. Both went down, linked in death.

Ruprecht loped forward, jinking around wild shots from the remaining soldiers, as a pair of crescent-shaped blades snapped out from his forearms just beneath the elbow.

Tiberian grabbed a dead man by the ankle and swung hard, his armor struggling with the sudden demand. The body clipped Ruprecht's outstretched arms and deflected the strike away from Tiberian.

Ruprecht landed and slashed both swords at Tiberian. The Daegon swayed back and the edge clipped his breastplate. Tiberian raised his pistol and shot Ruprecht in the visor again. The bullet hit the seam of the front visor and the metal encasing the side and back of his head.

The Katar struck again, the projected arc of the cut too short to hurt Tiberian as he fired again.

Ruprecht's cyborg arm telescoped out and the metal crescent struck Tiberian's wrist and cut the hand clean off. The pistol fired again as it spun up in the air and the severed limb spasmed.

Tiberian hacked at Ruprecht and his sword caught the cyborg on the shoulder. The blade hacked off a rod connecting the scapula to the joint and Ruprecht slunk away as the reverse stroke narrowly missed his visor.

Ruprecht—one arm hanging useless at his side—lunged forward and sliced a crescent blade up at Tiberian's neck. The cracks across his faceplate fouled his vision and Tiberian parried the strike. The Daegon kicked out and caught the cyborg on the knees, turning Ruprecht's landing into a fall.

"Abomination!" Tiberian reared back and hurled his sword at Ruprecht just as he sat up from his tumble.

The sword hit Ruprecht in the solar plexus, pierced through his back, and embedded against the floor, pinning the Katar in place. Ruprecht snarled and thrashed like a dog held at the end of his leash.

"Weapon," said Tiberian, holding out a bloody stump to a Daegon soldier. The two glanced at the injury, then Tiberian snatched the soldier's weapon away with his remaining hand. Tiberian flipped the rifle to full auto and shot Ruprecht's functioning arm around the shoulder, ripping it away.

Dropping the rifle, Tiberian looked down at his stump. The flesh darkened as the shorn end of his armor heated up and cauterized the wound. Injectors beneath his breastplate hissed as drugs pumped into his system.

"What are you?" Tiberian asked, approaching slowly. "Just a machine…or did you surrender all your flesh to become this…thing?"

Dark liquid spurted out around the blade impaled through Ruprecht's chest.

"Harl-harl-harl—" Ruprecht's voice box caught on the word and he snapped his head from side to side to turn it off.

Snatching Ruprecht by the chin, Tiberian squeezed until the visor cracked further and one side popped free of the housing.

The Katar emitted a slow, controlled laugh.

Tiberian gripped the edge of the visor and pried it open. He tossed the broken glass aside and looked down at Ruprecht's true face with disgust. There was no flesh on the Katar's skull. Red optics replaced the eyes and thin wires ran the length of the bleached bone.

"Pathetic." Tiberian thrust fingers through Ruprecht's optics and hooked his thumb under the chin. He ripped the Katar's head off with a snap of electric lines and the crack of failing metal then held the still-laughing skull at eye level before dropping it to the floor.

Tiberian stomped Ruprecht's head and the laughing stopped.

"My lord," said a soldier from the box where Syphax's limbs jutted out, "the inquisitor is dead. What shall I—"

"Take him to our garrison and have the body examined before it's returned to the *Sphinx*." Tiberian winced at the smell coming off his severed wrist. "I will report this directly to the Baroness…after I find a *chirurgen*. Where is my hand?!"

Chapter 21

Seaver lay on his side, cold sweat pouring from his body, pain needling him with every breath. Moving sent a wave of nausea through him and the dry ache in his mouth and neck from dehydration was a better constant than the agony he'd feel if he crawled to the fountain in his cell.

Through all this, he heard bird calls and the sound of children playing. Why he was hallucinating this was a mystery, but the joy of phantoms was the sole bright spot through his torment.

He felt a touch on his shoulder and a wave of cold spread from the port on his collarbone through his body. Seaver took a deep breath and the lights overhead grew painfully bright.

"On your feet," Juliae said.

Seaver sat up from his sweat-soaked mattress and blinked hard at the centurion. She was in full armor, hands on her hips, a dull smile on her face. All the burns were gone, her purple countenance just like new.

"Master?" Seaver touched his injection port and a pleasant warmth spread through his muscles.

"Don't make me repeat myself," she said, "else you'll…taste the back of my hand. Which has a bit of a spicy flavor. That's bad, by the way."

Seaver squinted at her, unsure if he was dreaming. A Daegon stood at the open cell door, confusion on his face as well.

Juliae's nose dropped, the tip almost reaching her upper lip when she waggled a finger beneath it and set it back at a bad angle.

Seaver scratched his nose and Juliae fixed her face.

"Come now, my favorite slave…I'll not have you dressed like that." Juliae looked back at the guard and he tossed her a set of clothes vacuum-wrapped in plastic. Juliae didn't try to catch the packet, which bounced off her shoulder and landed at Seaver's feet.

"Is that how you treat a centurion?" Juliae asked the guard. "Away with you! Bring food for the rest of my themata. They look famished." She flung a hand up to dismiss the guard and held it high as the Daegon lowered his chin and left.

Tolan looked up at his hand and his face went slack, like a sheet that needed to be tucked in.

"I…am having some trouble," he said.

Seaver slipped on a plain set of fatigues and stuffed his feet into boots stowed beneath his cot.

"What's going on?" Seaver asked. "Why am I…and you…"

"This is a jail break." Tolan grabbed his raised arm and forced it down. "I have changed my face wa-a-a-a-ay too many times in the past day and now I'm going a bit loosey-goosey. Need you to…" He reached behind his cape and a pack of cigarettes fell to the floor.

Seaver pulled the straps on his boots and sprang to his feet.

Tolan was bent over the pack, one hand scraping at the floor as he tried to pick it up. "Little help here," Tolan said.

"What's wrong with you?" Seaver scooped up the pack and lifted Tolan up. The spy came eye to eye with Seaver, which didn't match the true centurion's stature.

"I'm melting," Tolan said, pushing the corners of his mouth up into a smile. "Melting…need the stick with a green band around the filter. Just jab it in my throat. Hurry before that pig gets back here."

"OK, OK." Seaver jiggled the pack and a cigarette with the right marking came up. He poked the tobacco end against the spy's throat.

Tolan's face dropped and his eyes looked at him like he was some kind of idiot. Seaver flipped the cigarette around and jabbed again, earning a snap-hiss from the injector.

"That's the stuff." Tolan's face tightened and his visage shifted from Juliae's to Seaver's mother.

Seaver yelped and dropped the pack.

"Wait, no, that's not right." Tolan pressed a fingertip to his temple and his face returned to Juliae's. "All better," he said, his voice going back to the centurion's. "You and I are both on borrowed time, buckaroo."

"Why's that?" Seaver pocketed the pack.

"Because I hit you with an impressive cocktail of amphetamines and dexadromone. Do your teeth feel a bit fuzzy?"

"Now that you mention it…" Seaver touched his mouth.

"You're a big boy now. I don't know how long it'll take your body to metabolize everything, and the come-down from that stuff is a bitch…I've heard. Let's go." Tolan spun around and walked into the bars.

Seaver turned him toward the open door and guided him out.

"But the others?" Seaver looked over his shoulder to the cell with the few remaining survivors of his themata.

"Juliae gives a crap about them?" Tolan asked.

"No…"

"Then I can't either. Resources were put into you, kid. The rest are just chaff off your wheat." The spy turned a corner and froze.

"Oh," Tolan said, "Legio Keanu. Key-oh

307

no…what a surprise." He raised a hand slightly and stopped Seaver before he could come around and be seen by Keoni.

"Master," the legio said as Seaver glanced back at the cells…and the absence of any other way out of the holding area. "Master, I not hear release from *ho'opono*…you are shorter now. Your face…"

"Think we're past the point of no return," Tolan said. "Little help here?"

Seaver shouldered Tolan into the wall and kicked Keoni just above the knee. His shin whacked against the legio's leg armor, knocking him off-balance.

Seaver snatched the shock maul off Keoni's belt and flipped the grip. He raised it up to strike the legio on the head, but the maul activated and sent an electric line down his arm and into his chest.

Keoni swore in his native language and punched Seaver in the face. Metal studs on his knuckles ripped across Seaver's chin, leaving two bloody lines.

Using his bulk, Seaver lurched forward, putting both hands on Keoni's chest and shoving him backwards. Keoni's feet left the ground, his skull cracking against the wall, as Seaver kicked out and caught him in the ribs before he fell to the ground. With blood and spittle dripping from his chin, Seaver kicked and stomped the unconscious Keoni as months of frustration and anger boiled over.

"Kid. Kid!" Tolan pulled Seaver back by the collar. "I love a good beatdown as much as the next guy, but we've got a ride to catch."

"He's still breathing." Seaver jerked against Tolan's grip, but the augmented strength in the armor held him back.

"Imagine all the trouble he'll be in when your boss lady finds out, yeah? Let's say it'll be a fate worse than death and get going." Tolan reached for a door handle to a stairwell and missed.

Seaver got the door open and led Tolan away by the hand, heading down the stairs until Tolan yanked him back.

"Up." Tolan held up a finger and went cross-eyed staring at it.

"We get to the roof, we'll be trapped," Seaver said.

"We'll fly away," Tolan said. "Can I morph wings and carry you away if I need to? I don't want to find out." He looked at a wrist then the other that actually had a lit screen with a timer on it.

Leaning back against the stairwell, Tolan's skin went to a frog-like shade of green as purple dots formed and dissolved across his skin.

"You OK?" Seaver asked.

"I am not," Tolan said evenly. "I…am in overdose territory with my Bliss. I can't move my legs."

"Damn it." Seaver squatted down and pulled Tolan over his shoulder. He stood, his muscles shaking under the weight of the man and the armor, and started up the stairs.

Whatever drugs Tolan had hit him with tapered off after he'd made it up four floors and his legs went to rubber. Seaver stumbled against the railing, almost dropping Tolan down the stairwell.

"Kid…the hell? Kid…" Tolan's voice came out in differing octaves.

"Almost there," Seaver said and kept going, each new step harder than the last as his muscles burned with acid. He closed his mind off to the pain and took the steps two at a time.

He got to the top floor and reached for the handle, when a bullet snapped past his head and cracked against the ceiling. A whine of engines rose through the door as Seaver ducked and flung the door open, bullets whacking against the door as they got out onto the roof. Seaver slammed the door shut and glanced around.

Tolan rolled onto his back, his face going slack and drooping like a tablecloth over his skull. Seaver yanked a knife off Tolan's breastplate and jammed the blade into the hinge.

The sun had fallen just below the horizon, dark silhouettes of buildings standing out against bands of orange and red of the sky's last light, as the *Joaquim* came overhead, her engines buffeting the two men and drowning out all other sound. The ship spun around, and the lowered rear hatch with Dieter and Geet came into view.

Geet raised a carbine at Seaver, but Dieter pushed the muzzle down and slapped the man on the back of the head.

"Almost there," Seaver muttered, ignoring the pain throbbing across his body as he dragged Tolan toward the ship.

The *Joaquim* dipped suddenly and the edge of the ramp bounced off the roof, almost crushing Seaver. Slapping his hands against Tolan's shoulder, Seaver tossed him like a sack of potatoes onto the ship then reached for the ramp as the ship rose up. He gripped the steel grate and held on as the ship lifted up and away from the building.

As his feet came off the roof, panic blossomed through his heart when the ship angled up.

"Help!" Seaver tried to pull himself up, but his strength was ebbing.

The ramp buckled and the hydraulics whined as it began to close with Seaver still half dangling over the edge.

Dieter grabbed Seaver by the wrist and hauled back. Seaver struggled to gain purchase on the metal until a boot toe hooked on the ramp and he pushed himself up and into the ship. The ramp snapped shut and the roar of engines went mute.

"Why are you so big?" Dieter asked. "So

heavy but so weak?"

"I love this ship," Seaver said, still flat on his stomach, and gave the deck a gentle pat. "Even though it smells like piss."

Tolan sat up, his face back to his base shape of a man in his late thirties with shallow features. He looked around like he wasn't sure where he was, then hooked a thumb under one side of his breastplate and the armor fell away with a snap. The spy shrugged his way out of the plates and got to unsteady legs, wearing only a pair of undershorts. His skin drooped like a once-obese man that had lost weight rapidly and unnaturally.

"Oh, put a shirt on," Dieter said.

"Really?" Seaver raised a hand. "You could've dropped all that shit before I carried you to the roof."

"Builds character." Tolan made his way to the bridge and stopped at the stairs leading up. "Stealth drive?"

"Useless this close to the surface," Dieter said. "We need to get up to at least—"

The ship bucked and the nose rose higher. Tolan struggled up the stairs and practically climbed into the co-pilot's seat on the bridge.

Loussan's jaw was set firm, both hands on the controls. He didn't even look at Tolan as he buckled himself in.

"I hate you," the pirate said. Ahead, Albion's horizon fell away. "No radar or lidar. The Daegon fighters vector in on us and we'll be dead before we even know they're here."

"I put the skies in chaos before I left Orbital Command," Tolan said. "Planted several tiers of scrambler viruses in the deep computer servers. Soon as we activate the stealth drive and..."

"Here goes nothing." Loussan raised a plastic cover and pressed a red button three times. The lights beneath the panels and the ceiling dimmed and the sky ahead of the ship went sepia.

"We didn't explode...small favors," Tolan said, removing a clip from behind an ear and plugging a data drive into a port. "We need to get to Lantau. Slip equation's uploading now."

"Lantau? Why the hell we going to Kong space?" Loussan asked.

"You have warrants there?" Tolan asked,

slinking back against his seat.

"I have several death sentences." Loussan's face went red.

"Naughty, naughty." Tolan wagged a finger. "I owe you…your identity's safe with me. But Lantau's where we should find Gage and the fleet."

"'Should'? Did you say 'should'?"

"New Madras is still under threat from Daegon attack. Gage wouldn't stay there. Lantau's the next major system away from these assholes. I got a fairly good look at the Daegon's force disposition across their occupied territory…they're massing against Lantau. We need to get there before them."

"I sacrificed Ruprecht for this," Loussan said. "Tell me you got something worth his loss for this trip to a jackboot world."

"The head of the Albion Intelligence Ministry died—or at least I hope he's dead by now—to get me inside. Then there's all the innocents who'll die in the mess of the bombings and chaos in the skies. So yeah, I hope I got something worthwhile too." Tolan reached into his mouth and yanked out a tooth. "It's here…the slip equation to Epsilon Tau-Exi and the

Oculus."

"The what and the where?" Loussan asked.

"A choke point, you filthy pirate. It's a choke point back to the hell pit the Daegon climbed out of." Tolan gripped the tooth hard. "We have to destroy it before their next armada gets through…if we fail, the war's as good as lost. And we don't have long to do it."

****

Tiberian stood with the end of his severed arm in a long box. A medical droid with long metal arms hovered over the box and jabbed at the stump, weaving flesh and material from tanks attached to its back into new bone onto a metal lattice.

Cleon stood behind Asaria, the inquisitor's shoulders hunched, a slate clutched in his hands. The Baroness had her hands on the pommel of a sword, its tip stuck in the floor of the otherwise empty medical facility.

"And there is nothing more to be learned from this Katar?" she asked Cleon.

"It is a highly modified cyborg," Cleon said, "but the cranium contained no computer cores or storage devices. We're tearing the city apart to retrace the path it took, but—"

"It was a distraction," Tiberian said as the robot finished attaching bones to his new hand. The metal arms snapped back to the wrist and began threading nerves and veins onto the bare skeleton. "Meant to lure Syphax away from something else. What?"

Asaria turned to Cleon, the metal of her armor forming talons down her limbs.

The head inquisitor cleared his throat slightly. "The Faceless was in the orbital control center. He accessed the systems and introduced a number of malware programs that we're still cleaning out. Void Master Calixta was killed in the confusion following the bombings."

"He knows," Tiberian said. "He knows about the Oculus."

Asaria's face darkened.

"There was an unsanctioned slip transit a few hours ago," Cleon said. "A back trace on the equation leads me to believe they were going to—"

"Lantau," Tiberian snapped.

"Yes. To Lantau," Cleon said. "A search of impressed vessels in the spaceport yielded one discrepancy: a ship that came in from Concord carrying a wounded centurion."

"Albion remains a problem," Asaria said. "Competent officers. Competent intelligence agents."

"Lantau is where their League meets," Tiberian said. "If they learn of the Oculus—"

"It won't matter," Asaria said. "They can't act in time to stop the next transit."

"We have assets in place to deal with the League," Cleon said.

"You had assets in place to control this planet." Tiberian half turned to the spymaster and the surgery droid beeped a warning. "How much faith should we have in you for someplace as far removed from our grasp as Lantau?"

"We are so close," Asaria said, "so close to finishing our writ…"

"Let me go to Lantau," Tiberian said. "Give me the ships we have in orbit right now and I will finish off the Albion and end the League."

"No," Asaria snapped. "No. If you take the garrison, we're vulnerable here. We must hold Albion and the Oculus system until the other Houses arrive."

"They're ferals." Tiberian flexed his new hand as the droid wove muscles and tendons. "They're on the edge of collapse. One final push and—"

"No." Asaria lifted her chin slightly. "We will not bleed more than we have to make the other Houses' writs any easier. Our task is nearly done. I will not jeopardize our future."

"Then the Faceless will pass on what he's learned to Gage and—"

"And nothing," Cleon said. "I have assets in place."

"I have a new writ for you, Tiberian," Asaria said. "The Oculus is vital. You will take a contingent to reinforce our position there and ensure the gate remains open for the other Houses. Then you will escort them to Albion and I will let the combined might of the Daegon loose upon the ferals. Time is on our side. Victory is ours…Gage and the others just don't know it yet."

"I am a hunter, not a garrison commander," Tiberian said, pulling his arm out of the box and looking up and down the new, glistening flesh.

"Patience, my love," Asaria said. "Cleon gave me his assurances. Don't you trust him?"

"Call me suspicious of the inquisition." Tiberian squeezed his new hand into a fist. "There is blood between me and the Albion. I want to balance the scales."

"Soon…soon." Asaria ran her fingertips down his knuckles. "Bring me the rest of the Daegon fleets and I'll let you loose. I need a patient hunter, not an angry dog that's slipped his leash."

Cleon touched the box at his neck. "On my life, the Albion at Lantau are doomed," he said.

"You'd best be right," Asaria said, "for your sake."

Chapter 22

Tolan looked at a face in the mirror. The discordant mass was ugly—a crooked nose with one drooping nostril, unlevel eyes, and differing blotches of pigment color. Patches rose and fell like the underlying flesh was on a slow boil.

The features tightened as he concentrated on the face he was born with until the skin went flaccid like an elderly man's.

His mind buzzed with the come-down from the cocktail of drugs he'd been on while on Albion. He ran fingertips over glass vials in his leather case…his body aching for the contents.

"Maybe a bit of a break, yeah? Long time in slip space to recover…"

There was a knock at his door.

Tolan slammed the lid shut and he whirled around, one hand on the case as the other went for a pistol tucked into the back of his pants.

"What?" the spy asked as he glanced around for a place to hide his case.

"Kid's having trouble," Loussan said through the door. "I'm not getting near that freak. He's *your* problem."

"Be right there." Tolan reopened the case and picked up vials one at a time. "No. No. He's not covered in imaginary ants, so that's a no…this one?" He swirled around a red liquid filled with golden flecks. "Guess this counts as a special occasion."

Slipping the drug and an injector into his pockets, he went out to a berth two doors down from his quarters.

Geet, Dieter, and Loussan were in the cargo bay. The three men looked up at him with expressions that didn't convey trust or confidence.

"He'll be fine…" Tolan waved them off and cracked the door to Seaver's room. A smell of body odor and ammonia wafted out.

Seaver lay on a cot, soaked through with sweat. The man was on his side, facing away from the door, naked but for a pair of shorts. His arms were wrapped around his midsection, and he shivered in the hot air.

"Kid?" Tolan closed the door behind him. "You eat something yet?"

"Go away," Seaver croaked. "Just let me die."

"Can't do that." Tolan moved closer and grimaced at Seaver's bulk. His muscles had been grown without an eye to aesthetics or natural proportions. The Daegon had dumped growth hormones and steroids into him and produced something blunt and brutal. "You carried me past the finish line. I'll get you home to free Albion ships and your mother. Keep that goal in mind, yeah?"

"The Daegon said…said I was bound to Juliae. Had to have her to keep me from…this. It hurts, Tolan. Everything hurts," Seaver said.

"Drugs are hell, kiddo," Tolan said, sitting near Seaver's head. "Sometimes you think you're just dabbling for a bit of fun or to make the pain go away…and you invite a demon into your body that has its own plans for your future. You didn't have a choice with what happened to you. When you're to blame, the pain can be almost cleansing."

"You enjoy it when your fucking face melts?" Seaver groaned and squeezed his midsection tighter.

"Nope. I sold my soul to take down a bigger devil. Turns out it amounted to a giant pile of nothing when Ja'war didn't face proper justice and those behind his crimes won't ever be exposed or brought to task. The Daegon upended everything...now I'm a bargain-bin shapeshifter with a slew of chemical habits without the top cover of the Intelligence Ministry. At least Gage kept me gainfully employed...but sometimes a curse is a blessing in disguise. I'll keep telling myself that." Tolan gave Seaver a pat on the shoulder, then frowned at the sheen of sweat he picked up and wiped his palm down his pants leg.

"And what...what about me?" Seaver asked. "What'll happen to me? I fought for them. Killed for them."

"I'll put in a good word with Gage," Tolan said. "If it weren't for you, Gage wouldn't know about the Oculus. Won't know what's coming for us."

Seaver hacked and spat out phlegm. "Doesn't matter for me," Seaver said. "Even when we get to Lantau…won't be a Daegon med station to fix me."

"You said you're DNA-linked to Juliae, right?" Tolan asked. "I've got her on file." Tolan rubbed his thumb down his fingertips and his hand morphed to match the centurion's. "Her DNA's in my marrow. I don't have the expertise or equipment to replicate whatever the Daegon were shooting you up with. But the *Orion* will."

"Liar," Seaver said, rocking back and forth. "Liar, you don't know what they can do."

"I know parents," Tolan said. "Your mother will pull out all the stops for you, kiddo. Now…I've got something that'll take the edge off." He screwed the vial of red and gold into the injector and it hissed as he primed the trigger.

"No." Seaver looked up at Tolan, his face a mask of pain. "This demon's enough. I don't need another one. This withdrawal will kill me before we make it to Mom or it won't."

"You're tougher than most," Tolan said, laying the injector on his lap. "Stay with us, champ. Me? I know what I am." He lifted the edge of his shirt and pressed the nozzle into his side, gasping slightly as the substance entered his bloodstream.

Tolan leaned against the bulkhead and looked down at the shivering soldier next to him.

"Just stay with us, kid. Stay with us."

****

Gustavus waved a palm over a sensor deep in the bowels of the *Sphinx* and a hospital door opened. The smell of necrotic flesh stung his nose as he approached a bed in the middle of the small room. The walls played holos of mountain vistas and prairies from Old Earth.

A damaged set of Daegon armor was on a T-shaped rack, the metal burnt and dusted with remnants from the last battlefield.

Juliae lay on the bed, lines leading from ports on her arms and neck into equipment and sensors beneath the mattress. Her hair had fallen out in clumps and much of the skin on her face was blotchy and leaked pus from open sores.

Gustavus leaned over her and her eyes fluttered open.

"I like your scars," she rasped.

"Nothing compared to what you've earned." He sat on the edge of the bed and lifted a hand to touch her forearm, then pulled it back.

"Ferals…had a nuke." She smiled slightly and a line of blood ran down her cheek from the corner of her mouth. A mechanical arm popped out of the side of the bed then folded over to spritz her face with antiseptics and dab at the wounds.

"I heard what happened and…you just had to be on the front lines, didn't you?" he asked.

"That's…where all the glory was. Lord Nicias knew what I did. He…sent me back for treatment, personally. Your father…your father will be impressed with me," Juliae said.

"He's dead." Gustavus looked away. "Died with his writ unfulfilled. My standing with the House is diminished. I am the son of a failure, but the Baroness didn't send me to the golems. There's that."

"Eubulus is gone?" Juliae raised a trembling hand and touched Gustavus' arm. "But now I'm such a mess...do you still want me?"

Gustavus took her hand gently. "I do...but you are without a House name. Even with Father gone, I can't take you. The Baroness will never allow it, and I am in no position to ask for favors, not after the loss against the Indus."

"Then I will not let this feral poison kill me," she said. "My themata will be redone. I will...win all the glory I need for the House to adopt me."

"Yes," Gustavus said, scratching at his scars, "about your themata...your last shaped was involved in an incident with the ferals."

"Then have him killed." Juliae coughed, her face momentarily a mask of pain. "Have him put down like a dog."

"That won't be so easy." Gustavus ran the side of a finger down an undamaged part of her face. "The inquisition will be here soon to ask you questions. Here's what you need to say..."

Chapter 23

Dr. Seaver ran a flesh knitter down a raw scar on Gage's arm. The rest of med bay was empty, though Thorvald's armor stood at the doorway, arms slightly elevated to its sides.

"You're responding very well to the treatment." The doctor raised the knitter and ran a hand through hair that had gone gray in the past few weeks. "I doubt there will even be a scar once all's said and done. Just avoid being stabbed by more pirates in the interim. That's my professional advice."

"Much appreciated," Gage said. "Is that blood test done?"

Dr. Seaver narrowed her gaze. "DNA matches off a dried sample isn't a request I'd ever thought I'd get from you, Commodore…maybe Tolan, if he was still around." She moved away from the exam table where Gage sat and went to a screen.

"It's a private matter," Gage said.

"I'm a medical professional," she said, scrolling through test results. "Confidentiality comes with that…hmm, you're a match to the sample. Same father. Are congratulations in order?"

Gage looked at the Genevan armor, then back to the doctor.

"Keep it quiet, please," Gage said.

"Yes, sire," she said. "All the scuttlebutt we've heard about the 5th Fleet is true? More Albion Navy to bring back into the fold?"

"It won't be as easy as on New Madras," Gage said.

"There's no Daegon ships lording over them…getting them out of here should be easier than slipping away from the Reich," Seaver said.

"Should be," Gage said, "but we're not going to assume everything will go easy."

"Albion fighting Albion," she said. "Has such a thing ever happened?"

"No…and if it does, it will be under my watch." Gage slipped his jacket back on.

"I wonder about my son." The doctor crossed her arms. "He's a fighter. Would the Daegon force him to fight against us? Or is he so proud that they'd never take him alive…"

"What do you hope he did?" Gage asked.

"I want him to live," she said. "There's always hope so long as you're alive."

"Good. Good way to look at it," Gage said. "Stay ready, doctor. I fear you'll be busy despite my best efforts."

"Boring is good," she said, shrugging, "but it's not up to me, is it?"

Gage left and the armor followed without a sound.

****

Gage looked over the holo on the bridge, double-checking the fleet's positioning.

"*Arjan Singh* has the last of the miners aboard," Price said.

Gage zoomed in on the spaceport and frowned at several large containers on the landing pad.

"What's with these?" he asked.

"The miners—and General Han—wanted to bring up the ore," she said. "Birbal refused. The material interferes with scanners and he said his ship is for war, not hauling ash and trash, as he said."

"I like him," Gage said. He directed the *Orion's* sensors to the landing pad and got static back. "Though this gives me an idea…Vashon, come over here."

"What are you thinking, sire?" Price asked.

"Insurance policy," Gage said, stepping to one side as Vashon joined him at the holo table.

****

Chief Dermott of the *Heracles* glanced over his shoulder and ducked down a dimly lit passageway. The lower decks of the battleship were normally quiet, and a great place to avoid the attention of overzealous officers and master chiefs. Getting away from the Daegon overseers was almost easier, as they'd yet to learn all the ins and outs of the ship.

He opened an unmarked door and slipped into a dusty closet. The smell of ozone and body odor greeted him as he sidestepped past server racks. He cringed at the obvious path he left behind him, but if the Daegon got wind of what he was doing, that would be enough. They didn't exactly need proof beyond a reasonable doubt that he was guilty. They'd just pop his torque and leave him to bleed out in front of everyone else.

Dermott squatted down next to a terminal and turned on a screen. Short text messages popped onto it: updates from the resistance throughout the 5th Fleet. His heart ached to read that the head contact aboard the *Thames* had been killed. He'd served with Chief Perry during his first cruise, back when the two of them had been fresh sailors. No more updates from the *Thames* after that.

He got to the more recent message and paused.

AIDAN LIVES // TORCH TORCH TORCH-A1

"You don't say…" He touched the Daegon collar around his neck. "Hell…it's about time."

Reaching behind the console, he pulled out a metal box and gave it a shake. He popped it open and his fingertips moved thin metal rods the length of his fingers back and forth.

"Not enough, but it's a spark." He pocketed the box and left.

****

Thorvald rapped on the door to the *Orion*'s chief armsman's office. A man with watery eyes and a long face looked up from his desk and gave Thorvald a once-over.

"What? You lost?" he asked.

"Thorvald, reporting for duty," the Genevan said with his best Albion accent. "I was drafted back into service on New Madras…I was no good on the gun line, so I got transferred to you."

"That right?" The armsman, Gersarch by his name tape, rubbed a sleeve across his face and took a small data slate from Thorvald. "What were you doing on that ice ball?"

"Security," Thorvald said. "I was Albion Marines long time ago."

"Been gone awhile, huh?" Gersarch asked. "We just call them Marines around here. You remember how to shoot?" He reached back to a rack of carbines and handed one over to Thorvald.

The Genevan slapped one side, unlocked the hinge, and examined the breach in one smooth motion. He swiped the tip of a pinky against the bolt and frowned.

"It's dirty," he said.

"Yeah. Fine. I needed another warm body to fill out my bravo team and you're it," Gersarch said. "Clean that up then grab a bunk," he said, jerking a thumb over his shoulder. "You're in Petty Officer Lowen's team. He'll tell you when we've got the shoot house for our next drill. You flunk out of there, I don't know where they'll stick you. Probably the mess hall, scrubbing pots if all the bots break down."

"I see." Thorvald looked down at the carbine and at the small duffle bag containing a change of clothes. "I'll do my best."

"Welcome," Gersarch said with a shrug. "This better than sitting out the war with the Indus?"

"My last dying breath for Albion." Thorvald picked up his bag and went to the barracks.

Chapter 24

Gage put his hands on the holo tank controls as the 5th Fleet came around Taisan.

"Go active with sensors," Gage said. "Keep void fighters close."

"Aye aye," Price said and data streamed into the tank. The 5th Fleet was in battle formation, shield emitters charged but not active. The 5th didn't slow as they came over the horizon.

Gage opened a hail to the *Heracles*. No answer.

"All ships," Gage said into a fleet-wide channel, "stay alert…you know your orders."

Admiral Nix appeared in the tank. "Commodore." She smiled. "A tremendous day for Albion. Greetings from the 5th."

"Nix…I need you to stand down. Accept a

prize crew from my ships to each of your bridges and confine all officers to their quarters. Then we can get out of here," Gage said.

"I'm afraid I can't do that," Nix said. "Perhaps we can meet in person. Discuss this away from any prying eyes and ears."

Gage felt an icy pit growing in his stomach.

"By my authority as regent, I am ordering you to stand down, Nix," Gage said, lowering a hand and signaling to his gunnery officer.

Nix's eyes darted to one side.

"You're targeting my ships," she said. "Albion ships have never fired on each other before, Gage. We're above this."

"Then stand down," Gage said.

"Your authority...means nothing," Nix said. "Surrender to me and the Daegon. Now. I can't ask you again." She swallowed hard and a tear rolled down her face.

"You don't need to." Gage cut the channel. "All ships," he said, "Operation Catapult in effect. I repeat, Catapult in effect. Treat them as the enemy. Open fire."

"Lord have mercy on us." Price crossed herself and the *Orion*'s plasma cannons launched green bolts at the *Heracles*.

****

Wyman sat in his cockpit and caught his flight helmet tossed up by a tech. He bent his head forward and slapped the helmet on, connecting his life-support lines as his canopy lowered.

"This…is bullshit," Ivor said on their wingman frequency from her fighter next to his on the flight deck.

"Any particular part?" he asked as he went through his pre-flight checks.

"All of it. Flying against our own people. Goddamn Kongs holding us responsible for what the 5th did. The Daegon. All of this is bullshit, Freak."

"Yeah, life's a bitch and then you die. You gonna have that stenciled under your kill tally or you going to get your head in the game?" He looked over at her through their cockpits and rapped knuckles against the glass.

She returned the gesture.

"Briar's on deck for takeoff," she said over the squadron channel.

"Sprint soon as you're clear," announced Commander "Marksman" Stannis. "Boss wants us to get eyes on the target ships soon as possible. There's a chance the Daegon have bombs on the hulls and that keeps the ships in line."

"What does the Commodore want us to do, shoot them off?" Ivor asked.

"Hot mic, Briar," Stannis snapped.

Wyman rolled his eyes and glanced at Ivor, who looked like she was cussing herself out in her cockpit. Her Typhoon rose off the deck with a blast from anti-grav engines and flew out of the bay.

"Freak Show on deck," Wyman said. "Albion's light burns."

"Carry the torch, Freak Show," Stannis said as Wyman launched out of the *Orion*.

****

"Incoming!" shouted the *Heracles* gunnery

officer.

"Forward shields up," Nix said as she mounted her holo platform where Megeth and Lucian stood in place of her XO. The Daegon watched her as she continued to issue orders. "Typhoons in the void. Keep them as interdiction until we've got our shield wall established."

Cruisers and frigates formed a line alongside the *Heracles* as fire from Gage's forces struck the energy shields up across their prows.

"Why so cautious?" Megeth asked.

"To give Lord Bardas time to arrive," Nix said. "We sent a signal back to our force in orbit over Basai. An in-system slip-space jump is simple for the Daegon, correct?"

"Why haven't you fired torpedoes?" Lucian asked. "What are you saving them for?"

"Look." Nix brought the holo to bear on the entire battle as the ship rumbled with strikes to her shields. "Gage has his destroyer screen in place. If I launch torps now, his smaller ships will clean them up before they can reach their attack phase. We close and hit him with spine cannons. A massed shot will disable the *Orion*. Kill Gage. The rest will surrender once Bardas is here."

"You're hesitating," Megeth sneered, putting a hand to a metal bracelet. "Start killing them, Nix."

"As you wish," she choked out as the torque tightened around her neck. She tapped out a command and torpedoes loosed from her ships and bent toward the *Orion*. The torque went slack and she ordered her fighters into the battle.

Lucian put a palm to a screen and overrode the lockouts. He pulled up the comm station's logs, then half turned and barked an order to a Daegon soldier. The soldier fired a single shot and a blue bolt struck the communications chief in the back. The woman slumped out of her seat and crumpled to the deck.

"No message was sent to Basai," Lucian said. "Bardas knows nothing!" He swiped two fingers down a screen and mashed a thumb against a reader. A box opened in the holo and a voice wave matching Lucian's tone as he spoke Daegon came up.

"Jenkins?" Nix turned to a station behind her and held out a hand.

An officer popped open his void suit and tossed her a small pistol. Nix swung the weapon around and shot Lucian in the shoulder. He went down with a yell, the voice tone in the holo echoing his pain.

"*Heracles!* Torch!" Nix ducked under the holo table and shot Megeth in the thigh, but the bullet bounced off her armor. "Albion's light burns! We cannot—"

The torque around her neck bit into her flesh and blood gushed down her chest and back. As she fell to her knees, her vision blacking out, she aimed her pistol at Lucian's face and shot him just above an eye. She dropped the gun as all feeling in her body cut out. Nix fell to the deck, a puddle of blood emanating from her, as her bridge crew charged the surviving Daegon.

They didn't last long against the soldiers and their machine guns. Those that weren't massacred by the barrage died clutching throats cut by their torques. But Nix succumbed to the darkness with the solace of knowing the *Heracles* was true to Albion, even if she had failed.

Chapter 25

Wyman opened and closed his hand around his fighter's control stick. Icons for the distant 5th Fleet appeared on his HUD as the ships came around Taisan. Ivor flew close to him, while the rest of the Cobras formed a long line with him on the far-left flank.

"They've got fish in the water," Stannis said as smaller icons for fighters emerged from the *Heracles* and two other ships.

"They've still got the old IFF codes," Ivor said to Wyman. "It's…it's the King's Own squadron. Jesus Christ, it's the King's Own."

"Relax," Wyman said. "Just because the King's Own used to have only pilots with five or more kills and were the best in the Albion Navy doesn't…doesn't mean it's the same squadron."

"You're not helping me feel any better," she said.

"We're Cobras…honed fighting Daegon. That's an advantage they don't have."

"You're reaching, Freak. Reaching."

"You have something more comforting to say, be my guest," he said.

"*Orion*'s speaking with the other commander," Stannis said to the squadron. "Flights split into overlapping tracks. Hold position but stay frosty. Alpha, keep forward sensors on their Typhoons. They lock on, we are weapons free."

Wyman banked to one side and four other fighters joined him as he began flying a path that would take him into a long oval.

"Yeah…waiting," Ivor said.

"Talking's better than fighting," Wyman said. "Don't complain."

"You're not the boss of me. Now I can just sit here and go through worst-case situations while we fly racetracks."

"Anyone know pilots in the 5th?" Wyman asked the half squadron flying with him.

"I saw some of the King's Own once," said a pilot, call sign Boyband. "They looked like golden gods."

"Three from my class at flight school went to the *Thames*," Ivor said. "I do not want to shoot them. I also don't want them to shoot me. Who else loves their job?"

"Focus," Wyman said. "Hope for the best but stay frosty."

Ivor grumbled as they continued their track through the void. Wyman looked between the HUD icons for the other fighters and his load-out, wondering if he really could pull the trigger on other Albion pilots.

****

"Heavy damage to the *Ajax*," Price announced as Gage redirected his destroyer screen to compensate for the loss of the *Foil*. "Fifth ships—I mean the enemy is closing on spine-cannon range."

"Gunnery," Gage called out. "Ready the phalanx."

"Aye aye!" came from the bridge.

"There won't be anything left of them," Price said. "Why are they still fighting us?"

Damage reports from across Gage's fleet trickled in as plasma bolts crisscrossed between the two fleets converging on each other.

"Because they don't have any choice," Gage said. "Guns, priority target the *Heracles* and...wait."

"Fifty seconds to spine-cannon range," Price said. "If we trade fire with the *Heracles*, we'll—"

She stopped as Gage zoomed in on the other flagship.

"Their forward batteries have stopped firing," Gage said.

"Because they're redirecting energy to the spine cannon," Price said, a hint of fear in her voice. "Commodore, we need to...capacitor spike. Brace!"

A ripple of energy ran down the *Heracles*...and a cloud of shimmering dust spat out the cannon muzzle.

"What's going on?" Price asked.

Gage marked priority targets on 5th Fleet ships with their guns still blazing.

"Hold fire on the phalanx," Gage said. "Disable the *Sedgewick* and her frigate escort. Cease fire on any ship whose guns are dead."

"They're…they're fighting the Daegon?" Price asked.

"And we can do them the courtesy of not making the task harder by shooting at them," Gage said. "Nav! Work up the slip-space equation right now."

****

"Torps!" Stannis shouted. "Active torps!"

Crimson lines stretched from the 5th Fleet toward the *Orion*.

"Guess that settles it," Wyman said as he banked toward the enemy ships and opened his payload bays. An anti-ship missile swung out and the trackers in the nose cone spun to life.

"Stay out of the line of fire between the cap ships," Stannis warned. "Targeting guidance coming in from the *Orion* now."

"King's Own vectoring in," Ivor said. "They'll be in weapon's range pretty damn quick."

"Alpha, target the *Heracles* and have the missiles use their onboard guidance systems. We can't guide them in," Stannis said.

Wyman flipped switches and twisted a knob. A yellow border popped up around his payload screen.

"Set," Wyman said.

"God forgive us," Stannis said. "Fire."

Wyman's thumb hesitated…then mashed down on the trigger. His Typhoon rattled as the missile launched away. Afterburners flared as a half-dozen missiles sprinted toward the *Heracles*.

His HUD flashed red as radar locked onto his fighter.

"Paint!" Ivor shouted. "We're being painted."

"Switch to anti-fighter missiles and stand by," Stannis ordered.

"Stand by?" Wyman jinked his fighter as the Cobras closed on the King's Own in an attempt to throw off any missiles the enemy might fire off.

"They're…the die's been cast, sir."

"You heard me," Stannis said.

Wyman watched as the anti-ship missiles flew in the midst of the King's Own and his jaw dropped as each missile was shot down.

"Oh boy," he said. "They are that good."

"Here they come," Ivor said as the King's Own accelerated. "Vampire! We've got vampire!"

Threat icons for anti-fighter missiles appeared in the HUD and a long tone sounded in Wyman's ears. He cursed and dove hard, his fighter ejecting flares and chaff canisters to defeat the missile trackers.

He grit his teeth as the missiles closed…and shot right past him.

"What the—?" Ivor asked.

Light flared as the missiles exploded.

"Call up," Stannis said and every pilot in the squadron reported in.

"Did they…did they forget how to shoot?" Ivor asked.

"No way our countermeasures beat every missile like that," Wyman said as he brought his fighter back up and into attack formation with the rest of the Cobras.

"Bet it would look that way from the *Heracles*…" Ivor said.

"I think they're pulling their punches," Wyman said.

"*Orion*'s pulling us back," Stannis said. "We're on close interdiction for the next torp salvo from the enemy…let's show the King's Own we can knock down tubes just as well as they can."

"I'll take this as a win," Wyman said.

"Torps!" Stannis put target priority icons on three missiles coming off the *Sedgewick*. "Get 'em, Cobras."

****

Megeth rubbed a sore leg as the stench of spilled blood filled the *Heracles'* bridge. The flow of data into the holo tank was almost too much for her to process. The two soldiers she'd brought in to help manage the battle were proving less than useful.

"Why didn't the spine cannon destroy the

Orion?" she asked. "Did the shot miss?"

There was a bang on the doors to the bridge and the soldiers raised their weapons. Sparks flew out from the frame as a cutting torch went to work on the bolts holding the door shut.

"What a waste." Megeth touched her bracelet and ran a finger across the surface, sending a kill command to every torque within fifty yards. The sparks died out.

"Confirmation from Lord Bardas," a Daegon soldier called out from the communication station. "He'll enter slip space at any moment."

"Tell him the Albion have failed as thralls. Kill them all. I'll order all Daegon personnel to abandon their ships as soon as Bardas arrives. Give him a clear shot at cleaning up the last of them," she said.

The tip of a crow bar broke through the seam of the bridge doors and wrenched them open. A canister rolled through the gap and Megeth ducked behind one of her soldiers.

The grenade tore apart the holo tank and shredded the soldier's upper body. The concussion knocked the inquisitor off-balance and she slipped in Lucian's blood, going down on her side, ears ringing.

She heard muffled gunshots as she crawled to the gunnery station. Bullets broke it apart before she could reach it and a kick to her back sent her face-first into the deck.

Chief Dermott, a pair of rods slid between his torque and his throat, stood over her, a smoky carbine barrel pointed at her face.

Megeth squeezed her control bracelet and Dermott winced as the toque bit into the front and back of his throat. A thin line of blood ran down his neck.

"Albion's light burns," he said as he shot her in the face and his torque bit deeper into the metal rods, bending them. He gagged and dropped his rifle, clutching at the device trying to kill him. He fell to his knees, his face full of pain.

A crewman jammed a set of heavy clippers next to one of the rods and snipped off the torque. Dermott pulled it off his neck and threw it against the bulkhead.

"What the hell, sailor?" Dermott asked.

"Sorry, chief," the man said. "Worked from back to front after that bitch turned the torques up to max, or whatever she did."

Dermott looked at the wrecked holo tank, then across the bridge that had been ravaged by explosions and gunfire. The comms station still had power.

"Tell the auxiliary bridge to take over the ship," Dermott said, stepping over bodies on his way to the last working screens. "I'll try and hail the *Orion* and tell the Prince that this ship is with him from now until our home is free."

Rebel sailors cheered at Dermott as they looked over their dead and kicked weapons away from fallen Daegon.

Chapter 26

Gage put knuckles to the chin of his helmet as the last of the 5th Fleet's guns went silent.

"Cease fire," Gage said. "Price, get me Nix or whoever's in charge of those ships."

"Slip disturbance!"

Gage watched in horror as a Daegon fleet appeared over Lantau's north pole and made straight for the Albion ships.

"We have an equation," the astrogator announced. "Nine minutes until we can enter slip space."

A green diamond appeared away from Taisan in the tank.

"The enemy will be on us in five," Gage said.

"Recall all fighters. Set course for the slip point at best speed. Gunnery?"

"Aye, sire. Retargeting!"

A hail came from the *Heracles* and Gage opened it in the tank. "Nix?"

A sailor with a bloody face greeted him. "Negative, Commodore," Dermott said. "She's dead...along with the entire bridge crew. You see the Daegon come to claim us?"

"I do," Gage said. "We can slow them down but—"

"Begging your lordship," Dermott said, "but slowing them down may not be enough. Is it true, sire? Do you have Prince Aidan aboard?"

"It's true," Gage said.

"Ain't that something...somehow, I'm the ranking officer aboard the *Heracles*. Daegon killed off all our leaders soon as they realized we'd turned on them. As such, I'm making a command decision," Dermott said.

In the tank, the battleship turned around to face the oncoming Daegon.

"This ship can fight just fine when we've the

right targets," Dermott said. "Battery crews are in place…the spine-lance team won't forget to load a round this time."

"Dermott, is it?" Gage asked. "There's no need to do this. We can get away from—"

"Further begging the lordship's pardon," Dermott said, "but this ship's got a black mark on her. Admiral Nix would insist and who am I to disagree? Tell the Prince…tell him we're sorry. Give the rest of us a chance to prove we're true to him."

A spinning blue square appeared over the mining site…where several more cargo containers were arrayed across the landing pad. Gage touched it and torpedoes rose out of long ore haulers and launched up at the Daegon passing overhead.

"Heh…guess all the rumors I heard about you are true, sire," Dermott said. "The *Heracles* will be the anvil. Thanks for the hammer."

The channel cut out.

"Sire?" Price asked.

"Get us out of here." Gage watched as the torpedoes they'd seeded on the planet surface ripped into the Daegon fleet, wrecking smaller themata destroyers and pounding the shields of two battleships at the heart of their formation.

He watched as the *Heracles* lurched toward the enemy and her spine cannon fired. The hypervelocity round ripped through a Daegon cruiser and struck the aft of a battleship. The shields faltered and a pair of torpedoes from the surface hit the weakened shields and broke the spine of the linked-diamond ship. The engines spun off and the forward sections went tumbling end over end.

Themata destroyers shot forward and converged on the *Heracles*, taking the brunt of the Albion ship's fire. The lead themata vessel faltered, fire billowing out of the flanks as it flamed out from within.

The crippled ship struck the *Heracles*' forward shields and came apart. Two more destroyers rammed into the *Heracles* and broke through the hull. The ships angled toward the dwarf planet, like a whale laden with harpoons succumbing to the depths.

"Godspeed, Admiral Nix," Gage said. "Albion will never forget you. I will see you and yours added to the roll of honor back home. And we will go back home. I swear it."

The *Orion* and the rest of the ships jumped into slip space.

Chapter 27

In his wardroom, Gage gathered with the *Orion*'s chief officers and the head-and-shoulder holo projections of others from across the fleet.

"Casualty rates aboard the 5th were…concentrated," Price said. "Most of those lost when the Daegon triggered the torques were the officers in the closest proximity to the inquisitors. The sabotage teams that shut down weapon systems and seized control of bridges were more senior enlisted sailors. They got the rods that kept the torques from killing them. Seems the Daegon only thought a threat of rebellion would come from the officers."

"That's consistent with the Daegon," Gage

said. "They think they're the only ones capable of ruling, and they saw our officer corps as the closest thing to their authority. I'm afraid," he said, turning to Han's holo, "that there are no individuals responsible for the actions of the 5th against the Cathay left to prosecute."

Han sneered for a moment, then his face went blank. "The Emperor will likely accept this," he said, "but you'll have to explain what happened to him. In person."

"It will be my pleasure," Gage said.

"Do know that the consequences of any and all conduct of your fleet will fall squarely on you once we return to Lantau," Han said.

"And you'll take care of the 'refugees' we rescued from Taisan?" Gage asked with a wry smile.

"Yes…no need to expand on them to the Emperor." Han looked down and then to one side.

"Of course." Gage walked down the length of the conference table. "As this war grows longer, the free ships and fighters of Albion have coalesced under the *Orion*. The 11th is stronger now than when the Daegon first attacked…but I fear we are the last of Albion's military. We are all, ladies and gentlemen, but we are enough. We will reorganize as best we can once we leave slip space and join with the League to retake our home world. We—this exiled fleet—are the torch. And we will bring the light back to our people."

"Conduct repairs as best you can," Price said. "Void dock facilities on Lantau will be at a premium. Dismissed."

She cut the holos and Gage relaxed ever so slightly. Price led the rest of the officers out, and Salis, clad as always in her armor, entered the room with Prince Aidan in tow.

The boy, a stuffed bear in the crook of an arm, ran over to Gage and hugged him.

"What's this?" Gage put an arm around his shoulders.

"We've got more good people with us?" Aidan asked, looking up at Gage.

"That's right."

"They're all from home…but none are my family, are they?"

Gage went down to one knee to look the boy

in the eye. "No, my Prince…there's no one from your family. I'm sorry." he looked at Salis, but her face was hidden behind her visor.

"My father told me that I have to be tough," Aidan said. "That Albion will always be strong so long as the family is strong."

"Your father…your father is right, my Prince. This fleet keeps fighting because the family—you— are brave. We fight for you, for our homes…we will never give up."

"But Ms. Salis and Mr. Berty say I'm too small to fight," he said.

"For now. Only for now. Let me fight in your place for now." Gage touched the rank insignia on his shoulder. "Then you will have these and then you'll fight for Albion."

"Is it hard being a condor?" Aidan asked.

"Harder than I ever imagined." Gage smiled. "But I'm getting plenty of practice. I'll teach you everything you need when you're old enough."

"You're like my older brother, Jared. Or Nathaniel."

"Am I?" Gage asked quietly. "I never had a

little brother growing up."

Aidan's eyes lit up.

"You need a brother more than a mentor, right now," Gage said. "We'll do more together, all right?"

"Can you take me to Lantau? I heard they have good food."

"Let me make sure we're welcome there before we plan an outing, OK?"

"OK...now tell Salis to let me have more ice cream for dinner."

"No nutritional value," Salis said. "The simple carbohydrates affect his sleep rhythms and then—"

"A little extra just this once," Gage said. "To celebrate the 5th coming back into the fold."

Salis grumbled within her helmet.

"Let's go!" Aidan ran out of the wardroom.

"Don't tell him," Gage said to Salis. "He will be the King. Only him."

Salis paused in the doorway and nodded.

Chapter 28

Gage, Birbal, McGowan, and Thorvald's armor walked out of the imperial antechamber to the Lantau palace. Yellow banners hundreds of yards long hung from the raised corners of the palace's roof, each so heavy that the strong breeze in the air barely sent a ripple through the fabric.

Drones flew overhead, blaring messages in Cathay as holo text rotated around their edges.

A battalion of troops in golden armor formed a cordon on either side of Gage and his group. Stone-faced soldiers with perfectly manicured, identical beards stared at them as they passed. Cathay tanks and anti-air emplacements were packed along the inner wall.

"Pleasant bunch," McGowan said.

"The mandate of heaven requires decent security," Gage said.

"There's a point," McGowan said, looking up at the screen of Golden Fleet ships at anchor high overhead, "where showing strength comes off as weakness."

"If you're trying to make me feel better for my paltry—but more exclusive—entourage, it's not working," Gage said.

"I know why I'm here." McGowan scowled. "I don't like it, not that it matters. What's necessary doesn't give a toss about my opinion."

"Appreciated, and now you'll get the chance to tell everyone you laid eyes on the Golden One," Gage said.

"No need; bloke's picture's all over the place," McGowan said.

Shin greeted them at a large curved doorway.

"You all got the protocol message?" Shin asked. "The Emperor's in a mood this morning, and if you foul it up, he'll get grumpy." The old man leaned close to Gage. "You won't like him when he's grumpy."

"We're versed," Gage said, putting a hand on his sword belt.

A line of red light emitted from over the doorway and swept over Gage and the others.

"Those pigstickers of yours are fine," Shin said to Gage and then motioned to the kirpan knife on Birbal's waist. "Not that we could get that one off your Indus pal."

"No," Birbal said, "you would not."

"But the carbine your Genevan has…" Shin held out a liver-spotted hand. "No."

"Give it to him," Gage said to the armor. It snapped an arm over its lower back so fast that Shin recoiled in fright. The armor detached the compact machine gun, spun it around lightning quick, and thrust the stock at the advisor.

Shin's face scrunched up like he smelled something off, then took the weapon. The unexpected weight almost made him drop it.

"You'll get this back on the way out," Shin said. "I'll be right back." He shuffled into a smaller door hidden in the wall behind him.

"That was easy," McGowan said, looking at the armor. "I thought your man would put up more of a fuss."

"I made things clear to him beforehand." Gage looked up at the high walls of the palace, noting the dragon motifs carved into the ivory-colored material of the façade. "He's not happy. Which is why he's so tight-lipped."

"Your Genevan's prowess is known," Birbal said. "He fought that Daegon hunter to a standstill...I saw the video the Reich's Marines took of the fight. But I doubt he could fight his way out of the heart of a Cathay palace."

"I came to the same conclusion," Gage said. "Birbal, have you ever met an emperor before?"

"No Neo-Sikh would ever place himself so far above others," Birbal said. "Some Indus presidents have had delusions of grandeur...but their Neo-Sikh bodyguards kept them humble."

"First time for me too," Gage said as the main doors opened.

Inside, a long chamber of simple stone tiles and more golden-armored soldiers led to a backless throne palanquin floating a few feet off the ground. A green carpet led from the door to the throne, where a young man in a pale-yellow gown sat, hands on his knees, a silk cap on his head.

The Emperor.

Beside him was a pudgy man in a simple robe with a thick black belt.

Standing on either side of the carpet were several rows of councilors in blue and white robes, military officers, and those who Gage assumed were prominent businessmen wearing finery that cost more than he'd ever make in a year.

"Stay on the path," Gage said. "One step off and we profane the Emperor's house."

"Can't he just build a new one?" McGowan muttered as they walked toward the throne.

When they reached a golden rod laid across the carpet, a guard beat the handle of a long spear with a wide blade against the ground. McGowan and Birbal went to one knee at the rod. Gage and the armor remained standing.

"Doesn't he know what to do?" the Emperor spoke in Cathay and speakers built into the throne broadcast his words in English.

"The *gweilo* acts as King for the Albion," the pudgy man said. "We should allow him to stand…as a courtesy."

Gage recognized the councilor as one of the many eunuchs employed at the Cathay court. Just why the Cathay kept to such an old, barbaric tradition was beyond Gage, but he wasn't there to understand them, just enlist their help.

"And the metal one?" the Emperor leaned forward slightly.

"A mercenary," the eunuch said. "Perhaps the Albion do not trust their own people enough. We don't have that issue, Son of Heaven."

"I am Commodore Thomas Gage, regent of Albion," he walked forward to the next golden rod, the armor behind him. "I am here to represent Albion with the League. We must bring the war to the Daegon. We must strike back."

"And just why have the Daegon attacked?" the Emperor asked. "My advisor Zheng insists that Albion must have antagonized the Daegon somehow. Why else would they have attacked?"

Gage narrowed his eyes slightly. "The Daegon have made it clear that they intend to rule every world and every human being they can reach," Gage said. "They are monsters. They've killed millions already and there is no negotiating with them. No reasoning. We must push them back or we will all die. You've heard what the Daegon do to any leaders they capture…"

"Rumors," the Emperor said, waving a hand at Gage. "False information they use to frighten planets into submission."

"Emperor," Gage said, lifting a foot to step closer, but a guard brought a spear down across his chest. "The Daegon have attempted to kill Prince Aidan many times. They let loose a Faceless aboard my ship. Chased him down on New Madras. They killed the rest of Albion's royal family. This is true."

Zheng leaned over and whispered into the young man's ear.

"And you brought a Reich ship to my domain?" the Emperor asked. "And now you have ships that attacked my people under your command?"

"Those responsible for that…crime have been

punished," Gage said. "The Reich recognize the danger the Daegon present. It was not easy to accept their help, but their actions saved many innocent lives on New Madras."

Zheng whispered again, his porcine eyes fixed on Gage as he stood up.

"And hosting you here sends a message to the Daegon, doesn't it?" the Emperor asked.

"Your supplies and repair ships are greatly appreciated," Gage said. "My fleet is in your debt."

"I'm afraid," said the Emperor as he sat back and an energy shield flickered in front of him, "that your presence is no longer of use to me. Seize the Albion. Spare the Indus."

The wide barrel of a pistol thrust out from between the guards and fired with a *bloomp*. A wad of gel hit the Genevan armor, and electricity crackled over the surface. The suit went rigid and fell face-first onto the carpet.

Gage went for his sword, but a guard in power armor grabbed him from behind and slammed him to the ground. He saw McGowan accosted by more of the Emperor's men just before a hood went over his head. After a sharp, stinging bite into one side of his neck, he blacked out.

****

Ivor tapped a wrench against the fresh armor plate on her Typhoon and took a step back to admire her handiwork. Sailors and techs worked around the *Orion*'s main flight deck, the planet Lantau visible through the force fields covering the open bay.

"You see that, Wyman?" She shook the wrench at the other pilot, who was working beneath his fighter. "You see what happens when you don't get shot up? You get your repairs done quick and you can skip off for a nice nap."

"You mean you can hand me the epoxy gun so I can get this seal replaced," he said, waving to a toolbox.

"Oh, I see how it is." She tossed the tube up and let it spin a few times before catching it. "I save your bacon *and* I have to do your work too."

"What?" Wyman wiped grease off his face. "Are we keeping track now? Because if there's a tally,

I'm pretty sure—"

"You're one up on me for shore leave," she said and handed him the tube.

"On the pirate world? Did you think I had a good time down there? Running around with that Faceless weirdo, Martians, and lowlifes all over—"

A warning klaxon sounded and a Cathay shuttle came through the force field and landed in the center of the bay.

"Another supply shipment?" Ivor asked. "I thought we got the last delivery an hour ago." She rubbed the small of her back. "Give me something to do. I don't want to carry any more cases."

"Now you want to help." Wyman chuckled. "Give me the turbo encabulator tongs. The sperving bearings are off."

"Right, right…" Ivor reached inside the toolbox and a metal bang sent her jumping back.

The ramp of the Cathay shuttle was down and soldiers in power armor and carrying rifles charged out. One leveled his weapon at Ivor and shouted at her. She put her hands up and laced them behind her head as another Cathay shuttle landed and disgorged more troops.

Wyman was thrown to the ground next to her and a boot put on the back of his neck.

"I don't know what you Kong assholes think you're doing," she said to the Cathay soldier in front of her, "but you're going to regret this."

THE END

The Exiled Fleet series continues in THE LAST DITCH!

FROM THE AUTHOR

Richard Fox is the author of The Ember War Saga, and several other military history, thriller and space opera novels.

He lives in fabulous Las Vegas with his incredible wife and three boys, amazing children bent on anarchy.

He graduated from the United States Military Academy (West Point) much to his surprise and spent ten years on active duty in the United States Army. He deployed on two combat tours to Iraq and received the Combat Action Badge, Bronze Star and Presidential Unit Citation.

Sign up for his mailing list over at www.richardfoxauthor.com to stay up to date on new releases and get exclusive Ember War short stories.

The Ember War Saga:

1.) The Ember War
2.) The Ruins of Anthalas
3.) Blood of Heroes
4.) Earth Defiant
5.) The Gardens of Nibiru
6.) Battle of the Void
7.) The Siege of Earth
8.) The Crucible
9.) The Xaros Reckoning

Made in the USA
Coppell, TX
25 January 2020

14974325R00207